THE DEVILS YOU KNOW

THE DEVILS YOU KNOW

M.C. ATWOOD

SOHO
TEEN

Published in the United States by Soho Teen
an imprint of
Soho Press, Inc.
853 Broadway
New York, NY 10003

Library of Congress Cataloging-in-Publication Data
The devils you know / M.C. Atwood.

ISBN 978-1-61695-788-9
eISBN 978-1-61695-789-6

1. Haunted houses—Fiction. 2. Supernatural—Fiction. 3. School field trips—Fiction. 4. Secrets—Fiction. 5. Interpersonal relations—Fiction. 6. Horror stories.
PZ7.1.A89 Dev 2017 DDC [Fic]—dc23 2017021386

Interior design by Janine Agro, Soho Press, Inc.

Printed in the United States of America

10 9 8 7 6 5 4 3 2 1

For Mom (I miss you) and Dad, always.
I love you more than you love me.
(I win.)

Part 6

THE LEGEND GOES LIKE THIS:

At the tender age of 17, Maxwell Cartwright Jr. lost his mind and turned to evil. His father had struggled for years to make the family farm viable, to squeeze life from the land. Neighbors all around him did this well, coaxing crop after crop from the rich Wisconsin soil. But Maxwell Cartwright Jr.'s father could not do the same, no matter how hard he tried. He resented their success. So much so that he refused to talk to them.

Then one hot, humid day Maxwell Cartwright Jr.'s father set down his plow in the middle of the field. He walked by his son, who was feeding the few scraggly chickens. He walked past his house and his wife, who was sweeping the porch. He walked to the barn, slow and steady, never turning his head. Unaware of the murder of crows in the trees, hundreds of hunched black birds, sitting in branches, looking on silently. He took out his shotgun.

And blew his brains out.

And that's when, they say, Maxwell Cartwright Jr. turned to evil.

He blamed his neighbors. He blamed the land. He turned, they say, like how meat rots in the sun. He packed his bags, left his mother to the bankrupt farmhouse and the withering acres with the boulder that overlooked the hills of Wisconsin, and disappeared. No one knows where he went.

But they knew when he came back. They say he appeared

like smoke one day, right on top of the boulder. Pure white hair, though he was still young, eyes pure black. They say no birds sang that day, that the sky turned dark, that twisters funneled up north, south, east, and west of him. That lightning struck all around him. With his mother long buried and the old farmhouse long succumbed to ruin, they say Maxwell Cartwright Jr. climbed atop a boulder and surveyed the land and cursed it. He made a promise: he would build a House.

A House upon this very spot.

The House would be his vengeance. A price the world would pay for abandoning him. A great and terrible House, crouching in the shadows, collecting souls, exacting revenge for the abuse he believed his family endured.

A House, the legend says, that would always win.

Excerpt from pp. 21-23, *The Collections of Maxwell Cartwright Jr.*

VIOLET

I'm alone in the hallway, which is good because holy crap he's texting *again*. And I just saw him. I roll my eyes at no one. I wish my eyeballs could make a groaning sound, too. I wish I could laugh about this with someone else.

I should absolutely break up with him. But that would mean I'd have to hurt his feelings . . . Or make a decision. My mom or dad would say something psychological about this—autonomy, agency, etc.

The thought of my mom and dad knowing makes blood rush to my face, and I actually get a little dizzy. The thought of ANYONE knowing . . .

Holy cow.

The bell rings and students stream out of classrooms in twos and threes. I turn to my locker and spin the combination like I just got here.

Ashley Garrett bumps into me and I say, "Sorry?" She looks at me, her face a blank, and then keeps walking.

I'm pretty sure I'm here.

I'm here, right?

My pocket vibrates and I check the screen. Thinking of u. Ugh. Please stop thinking of me. And spell words correctly. I almost find the courage to write that, but then Laurie sidles up to me. "Violet. You will not believe what You-know-who did to me today."

She thinks she's clever and wants me to acknowledge it.

I fake-laugh. I guess I can laugh if it makes her feel good.

I swallow down my conscience and choke only a little on my inability to handle any sort of conflict.

Laurie's smile is a bird of prey. "You know. Instead of Stacey Bagley?" She flips her dirty blonde hair behind her shoulders and takes a big breath in.

"Anyway, You-know-who tells me IN FRONT OF JACOB that I have something in my nose." She snorts and sticks her hands on her hips. "IN FRONT OF JACOB."

Oh, Laurie. I heard you.

What I say is, "No way!"

She nods up and down, eyes wide and glinting with the sparkle of indignation. Or maybe it's new eyeliner.

I lean in close. "That is sooo horrible!" I put on a look suitable for "horrible."

And then Stacey is there. "Hey guys!" Stacey has brunette hair to Laurie's blonde, but other than that, their hair is exactly the same. Bangs, length, everything. Eerie.

I've never once talked about myself with them. Not once. They've never noticed.

Laurie's eyes narrow. "Hey, Stacey."

I am getting that nervous tickle in my stomach that things are going south. So I do what I always do. I divert. Divert before disaster. Happy happy happy happy. Before either of them can say anything, I say, "Holy schmolies, did you see Gretchen's outfit today?"

They both lean in. That's right, Vultures, come taste this road kill. I lay it out for them, the pièce de résistance being these frankly awesome faux-fur boots that somehow make her look even more hardcore cool than she already is.

What I don't tell them: I love the outfit. I wish I could wear it. I look down at my black A-line skirt and pink sweater. Both from Forever 21. Both boring.

Stacey rolls her eyes. "What a complete freak."

And then the bell rings for lunch and we start walking.

Gretchen passes. Laurie and Stacey snicker, and I laugh, too.

That irritating acid poke of conscience wells up again, but I tell myself that Gretchen probably wants to be talked about anyway, so no harm done right? Probably.

My pocket vibrates again, and I sneak the phone out and look at the screen. Ur not thinking of me? ☺

I sigh. "I'll meet you at the table," I say to Laurie and Stacey.

I wonder if they'll save me a seat.

Ducking into the bathroom, I text back quick, Always thinking of you ☺ I'm not lying. I am always thinking about how to get rid of him.

Vibrate. Text: Meet tonite?

My parents are out of town and he knows it. I tap the phone against my leg and then try, Lots of homework.

Text: U be schoolgirl then. ☺

Honestly, he can't type out "you"? I should break up with him for that. In the bathroom mirror, I see my brown hair, brown eyes. I'm pretty, I think. Except for my chubby stomach. My wobbly arms. And my nose. And my entire face. And body.

I text back: Should I wear a uniform skirt?

My heart sinks even as I write it. What am I doing? Why, Violet, why? I should be excited. I used to be. I think.

He did choose me, after all. But I can only think about what a mess this is and how gross I feel.

I practically run out of the bathroom and then smack right into Paul.

Paul.

If Paul came with a soundtrack, the songs would be sung by angels. Angels who recognize how hot he is, much like themselves. If Paul were a car, it would be made of clouds; it would run on sparkles. If Paul would have me, I would have his babies. Eventually, you know, not right now.

Oh, Paul. Beautiful, beautiful Paul.

Paul says, "Sorry."

I say, "I know," and then inhale quickly because what am I saying? I try to bite back the words and my throat does something funny. I cough. Which makes me laugh. So now I am cough-laughing and I can't catch my breath.

It turns out that Paul's brown eyes crinkle at the corners when he is confronted with a lunatic. He pats me on the back, and I keep coughing and laughing, feeling hysteria well up through my whole body and shoot out of my eyes.

I choke out, "I'm okay," and then move to run the eff away from this. But I run into him again because he's changed trajectory.

Please kill me now.

Something falls to the floor, and Paul bends down quicker than I thought was humanly possible to pick it up. It's book-shaped, and therefore probably a book (I am a straight-A student and can recognize these things). I am desperately interested to know what this book is so I can read it and then run into him again. And then quote it. While wearing glasses. If he likes glasses.

Paul gives my shoulder one last awkward pat and then turns on a heel and walks away.

There you go, Paul, in your cloudmobile made of angels. I so wish you were coming over tonight instead of . . . *sigh*.

I shake my head and look around. No one is there, and the hallway feels super empty and hollow, so I hurry to lunch.

After lunch is civics, during which I sign up for a field trip to Boulder House, even though I've been there before. The school says seniors who go on the trip don't have to take finals. I like tests, really, but school feels way too complicated lately. So a sanctioned reason to skip? Yes, please.

Later, in math, I daydream, pretending the class isn't torture.

Scene: Paul runs into me and drops his book. I bend down to pick it up. It's a journal about me! Every page has flattering pictures of me . . . drawings, pressed flowers, newspaper clippings of my goings-on. I can see the blush work its way up his cheeks, but I put my hand under his chin and I move in to press his beautiful mouth against mine . . .

"Violet." Mr. Rhinehart stands over me now, hands on hips. "Care to share with the class?"

My own blush starts from my toes. I shake my head. No, I do not care to share with the class. He really is a jerk. And he's wearing a sweater vest again. No one with a sweater vest is allowed to be mean. No one.

"Come back to Earth, Bullock. This isn't your movie." His lips curl and he walks back to the board. People in the class snicker even though his movie reference is a thousand years old. I die just a little and stare at the clock, wishing I could go back to dreaming. But there's no going back.

When the bell rings, I walk to my car as slowly as I can. I guess I have to get ready for tonight. I guess I have to find a school skirt. I guess I have no backbone.

I get home and throw my books on the floor by the door. I wonder if my mom—a psychology professor—ever wore a Catholic schoolgirl outfit for my dad, a practicing psychologist. They'd probably say psychological things the whole time: "Betsy, would you care to speak in a loud voice to evince cheering? Please only do so if you feel empowered." "Yes, Matthew, I would. I am a sexual being and I shall begin cheering to satisfy my id craving in a healthy, consensual way."

I am grossing myself out.

After an hour, I still can't find a skirt like the one I'm supposed to wear and probably more importantly, I don't want to.

A thought rises in my head like the sun, like power . . . I will break up with him tonight. Is that the straightening of my backbone?

I will do it. Yes. I will break up with him tonight.

Later. When the doorbell rings, monkeys dance in my stomach. I will do it. Stay strong, Violet, stay strong. He's creepy anyway, right? My skin crawls when I think of him. Really, it has from the beginning. I don't think that's how it's supposed to be. It's not that way when I think of Paul.

I open the door.

He says, "You've been a naughty schoolgirl, haven't you?"

I sigh and my heart sinks. Bye-bye, backbone.

PAUL

"Hey, Paul," Trent says.

He smacks my shoulder, like we're friends. I mean we are, I guess. At least here. I hike the book up higher under my armpit.

Trent and I walk down the hall. I nod at the rest of our team when we pass. I remember to add swagger. I almost forget. I'm preoccupied because of the book.

Trent carries a basketball around with him everywhere. This is as stupid as it sounds. He thinks it makes him cool, but he's pretty much the only one who thinks so. Mostly he's a big asshole. It's sad because he has something to prove. I don't even like basketball that much. I even considered not playing because, believe me, it's not like I haven't heard the stereotype. Out loud. Near my face. But I am probably the best on the team, and I'll take my cultural cachet where I can get it. You have to survive, you know?

The book slips a little so I squeeze my bicep closer to my chest. This sucker's going to fall, and my arm is already getting tired. Trent will never stop making fun of me if he sees it. Because, you know, asshole.

We get to his locker and he hands me the basketball so he can put his own books away. "So, tonight, bonfire, right?"

He spins his combination. The book under my arm slips a little more.

"Hot chicks," he says and moves his eyebrows up and down like an idiot.

I try not to laugh. The same girls we see every day. And guess what? I'll still be the only black person there.

I stall. "I gotta ask my mom." The book slides to my waist and I'm squeezing everything now, even random muscles that won't help. I think about dropping the basketball. Then I could slide the book back up while Trent chases it. It makes me smile to think of him scrambling around like a rhesus monkey.

Trent's laugh interrupts my reverie. It's more of a bark—short but like way loud. "You have to ask Mommy?"

Whoops. I swallow. I mean, it's true, I have to ask my mom. She and I have plans. But I know better than to say that. The book is tipping backward now, so time for a fast exit. I shove the basketball into Trent's stomach and at the same time, spin and use my other hand to jam the book back into my armpit.

"Check you later," I say to him, sweat starting at my temples.

I hurry down the hall before Trent can catch me in any more stupidity.

Must put book in locker. It was a risk to bring it today, but I couldn't resist, even though I would have to full-on torch someone if they saw it. It's a weird little thrill, carrying it around. Makes me feel a little brave. And this book isn't even a fourth of it.

I turn the corner and run straight into Violet.

Pretty Violet. I swear, flowers and birds stick out of my eyes when I see her. She's, like, *really* pretty. Like from-a-different-time pretty.

I say, "Sorry," but I'm not at all because I felt her boob on my chest. She's so freaking soft . . . I will myself not to get a boner. That would be rude.

Violet says, "I know," and I think she may be talking to someone else because we're standing near the bathrooms, and I feel like a fool.

Stupid, Paul. Stupid, stupid. Feeling brave now, dork?

Then I notice Violet's face is turning red. She's having a

coughing fit. I pat her on the back and try to step away. She chokes, "I'm okay," but then smacks into me again.

Maybe she's on drugs. It might explain her eyes, darting around everywhere. Funny, I thought she was a goody two-shoes. I never see her at bonfires, which is pretty much the only thing anyone does around here for fun. You know those films about Midwestern small towns? They aren't playing. Bonfires are, like, a thing. Anyway, Violet is most likely not on drugs. She's wicked smart—which is insanely hot, though I'd never admit as much to anyone. Not while I have to get through high school anyway.

She also smells good . . . I lean into her to smell her more but then, holy god, I remember that I just felt her boob (accidentally!) and need to stop myself from doing yet another thing that is totally creepy.

But then I see Violet looking at the floor and my throat closes up.

The book.

Shiiiiiiit.

I scoop it up in one hand and give her one final pat on the back with my other.

My kingdom for a horse.

I turn and walk away as fast as I can without actually running. Flipping open my locker door, I shove *The Sonnets of Shakespeare* at the bottom of my pile of books as fast as I can. And then I breathe for the first time since I got to school. This book isn't even the one we're supposed to be reading for English class. I grab my actual English book and try to stop sweating.

I feel another boob on my shoulder.

A tingle shoots through me, I admit. Fie on all boobs, for Chrissakes. Boobs should be outlawed in this school.

It's Ashley. Way-hot Ashley. She bats her eyelashes at me. "Coming to the bonfire tonight, sexy?"

I wouldn't ever really go for her. I'm more of a Violet girl. But like I said, you have to survive, right? And Ashley? Dumb as it is, stupid and stereotypical as her M.O. is: She can make your life hell or keep you right in this school. I pegged it when I first moved. You find and friend the most ruthless; you keep your head down; you get through.

I turn fully to Ashley and lower my eyelids. I've practiced this in the mirror. It's my sexy look.

"Depends. Are you going?"

She licks her lips. She's a nymph, this one. Total dick-tease though, I've heard.

"Maybe." She turns on her heel and sashays away, looking over her shoulder once like a sex kitten in a slasher film. She looks great from the back, too. Maybe I will go to the party tonight. I think of boobs and wonder if Violet is going. And then realize I just objectified not one but two women and my mom would kill me.

Which reminds me that if I go to the bonfire tonight, my mom would kill me twice. Besides, the fitting is tonight and I can't wait to see how I look .

I slam my locker and head to English—so excited for this class—head nods from everyone.

Ms. Harper is writing "Now is the . . ." on the board when I slip into my seat in class, and my heart beats a little faster. I know this quote. I look around the room and see if anyone else is paying attention.

The final bell rings and the last stragglers slip in. Ms. Harper turns around and reads in deep dramatic voice, "Now is the dot dot dot. Extra credit for the person who figures out the rest of this quote by the end of the class."

So easy. "Now is the winter of our discontent." *Richard III.* I'll take that extra credit now, please.

Tracey, who sits behind me and totally wants me, taps me on the shoulder and leans into my ear from the back, "Now is the time for her to shut the hell up." Her breath tickles my ear, but not in a good way. Every part of me wants to give her a dirty look but I chicken out and snort instead. Better to play it cool.

Ms. Harper goes on. "Oh, but before we jump into discussing

the Bard, I want to talk about the upcoming Boulder House senior field trip. I am the lucky teacher who will be taking you! I'm just so thrilled—it's a magnificent place. So, a few things as I pass around this sign-up sheet."

I keep hearing about this Boulder House and the senior field trip there. I guess it's something the school does every year for seniors, only no one is required to go. It sounds mad stupid. And I still don't get what it is. Or why I'd go.

"First things first: if you go on this trip, you don't have to take finals." Ms. Harper says.

Well, that's one question answered.

"Second, the House . . ." Her eyes actually go starry. "Oh, the House, students. I consider this House poetry in motion. Maxwell Cartwright Jr.—the great man who built it—is an underrated architect of Wisconsin. You all know Frank Lloyd Wright, of course—" I look around and there are only blank faces "—but Maxwell Cartwright Jr. built a House basically IN a boulder. And on top of it. Architects to this day don't understand how the engineering of this House works and how it stays standing. Some say it's magic!"

She wiggles her fingers and makes her eyes wide. The class doesn't respond. I feel bad for her. Why, oh why did she ever want to teach high school?

But she keeps trying. "Anyway, Maxwell Cartwright Jr. went to this very school when it was only one room in the 1930s. Can you believe it? And it was more than just the junior high and high school combined: it was ALL the grades at the time. Anyway, it was still called River Red School, just like it is today. Maxwell Cartwright Jr. is our most famous alum!"

Tracey laughs behind me. "Uh, okay. So some old guy built this house. Who cares? Why is this our field trip? You know, some seniors actually go to Paris for their field trips. But we're stuck with a 'magic' House?" There are laughs all around in class. Why does she have to be so bitchy? Ms. Harper is trying. I don't say anything and just sit and burn.

"Glad you asked, Tracey!" Ms. Harper says. She walks near my desk and Tracey's behind me and her voice gets lower. "Well, if you want my opinion, you'll definitely want to go see the genius of Maxwell Cartwright Jr., but it's not just the House—his genius is in his collections. He has the biggest— and strangest—collections of things in warehouses attached to this magic House, you see. Every room has artifacts from around the world. Statues, animals, objects. The enormity of the place and the breadth . . . the depth . . . Well, it's inde- scribable. It's something you have to see to believe." She lowers her voice even more. "Some say these collections have a life of their own. And that Maxwell Cartwright Jr. was actually a devil or demon, always on the lookout for new souls to collect. But certainly that's just silly. Really, it's just an incredibly interesting place."

She winks at the class and then goes to the board again.

"But, I get it if you're not sold on the idea. As a student, the main reason to go is so that you won't have to do finals. What harm can it do?" She picks up a dry-erase marker. "Okay, back to the Bard! Anybody guess the quote yet?"

But I'm thinking of this House still. It sounds . . . nutso. But, like, interesting nutso. And because I believe education is important, I decide I want to go. My mom would want me to go. And maybe Violet is going . . . She seems like the field trip type. But most of all, in this moment, it will stick it to Tracey.

Tracey leans into my ear again, and hands me a piece of paper over my shoulder. "Here's the stupid sign-up sheet for the Boulder House. I swear, I wouldn't go on this if you promised me a million dollars. What are we, like, five? Who gives a shit about collections?"

She is the worst. Do I really care if she likes me? Sort of. Sort of not. I turn in my seat so she can see my profile, and grab my English book. I stick the sign-up sheet for the House on the book and sign my name. Slowly.

I look up at Tracey and smile and her face has frozen, her pen halfway to her mouth. I hand the paper to the person in front of me and have to hold in a laugh. I can almost feel Tracey's panic on my back, can feel her following the paper around with her eyes. Passive aggressive? Maybe. But I feel better.

Maybe some day I'll have the courage to . . . I don't know. Say what I think? Just be myself? But that's not going to be today. Sometimes I wonder what my dad would think of me. It's been eight years since the heart attack, but that day is burned into my head. And the fact that I didn't do anything—anything—to help.

Maybe being myself isn't a great idea after all.

But, like, whatever. I just know a person has to survive, right? I turn back around and lose myself in thoughts about the role-play coming up. I have a fitting tonight, so that'll be boss. A fitting for my other life and my other me. The one I actually like.

DYLAN

My days? Undercover, yo.

I come to school.

Duck behind the dumpsters.

Paint my nails black.

Change into my Anarchy (sometimes Sex Pistols) T-shirt, skinny jeans, Cons.

Put on the wallet chain.

Put on the black eyeliner.

Get knocked into a locker once I'm in the building.

Meet Gretch.

Today she's wearing this pimping cool fur outfit and I want to jump her right there. But with Gretch, you have to be subtle. So, I crawl my fingers up her arm and tickle her neck.

She knocks me with her math books, but I catch a smile.

"Why do you always smell like fingernail polish?" She keeps stuffing things in her locker and I pull my hands back quick, check to see if the polish is ruined. Solid. I use the quick-dry kind, like a drag queen western.

"We need to do your hair," I say, and pick at her roots. "I have some bleach left."

She sighs. Grabs the books she needs and shuts the locker. "We always need to do my hair. The problem with short bleach blonde."

I do a little tap dance number in front of her, even though I don't know how to tap. I say, "That's showbiz, baby!" And then I bow.

When Gretchen smiles, the crease between her eyebrows loosens up a little and the sun comes out. The sun shines full force on me now.

Then I get shoved into a locker. Again.

Trent, drone-bot asstroll school basketball god, says, "Freak," and spins that ever present ball in his hand. Paul next to him shakes his head, just enough so that only I can see. He doesn't say anything to Trent, though, like, "Hey douchejockey, maybe stop knocking Dylan into lockers?" He does, however, step just a little bit in front of Trent as they keep walking—just enough so that Trent has to veer, making him lose control of the stupid-ass ball. While Trent chases it, Paul turns around to me and gives me such a slight wink, I'd think I was imagining it if the timing wasn't so rad. Paul's cool. I don't know why he hangs with that asstroll, though.

But, holy uh-oh, I hear rumblings right next to me. The bear that is Gretchen is waking up. The crease is back. Her face is getting to eggplant purple. We're at DEFCON 5. She's a'gonna blow.

"Gretch," I say, but it's too late.

She screams down the hallway, "Overcompensating, Trent? One big ball doesn't make up for two tiny ones!"

Unless I can calm her the h-e-double-hockey-sticks down, I'll be sporting a black eye tonight. And God knows I don't want to explain a new injury to the Ps. It's happened before. See, Gretch will go and scream at Trent in the hallway, maybe even shove him—definitely get in his face—but who will he come after?

ME.

Luckily Paul has already dragged him around the corner. Class is about to start.

"Gretch, baby," I whisper, "why you using words you knoooow he don't understand? You gotta use one-syllable words."

Her face is back to its normal sunrise pink. She puts her hand on my head, pats. We are exactly the same height.

"Or I can just grunt," she says.

I chuckle, then make ape noises. Scratch under my armpits. Maybe take it a little too far when I climb up the lockers and bang against them over and over, grunting grunting grunting. I move close to Gretchen and sniff at her neck, bury my head near that soft spot under her jawline where her neck starts swanning.

"Baby?" she says. Irritation Lite-Brites under her voice. Yeah. Too far.

"Yeah?"

"If that fucker runs into you again today, punch him in the throat."

She tucks her books in her bag that looks like a monster. Like, it has monster eyes on it. And teeth. I love it. Like I love her. I can't help myself. I burrow under her jawline again, give one more ape noise grunt. She backs away, heading toward class.

When she turns around, she yells, "The throat!" and the second bell rings.

And I haven't gotten my books. Tardy again. Wuh-oops.

I try to slip into Mr. Rhinefart's room without him noticing. His real name is Rhinehart. Scratch that. His REAL name, like who he really is? Definitely Rhinefart.

He says, "Well, Dylan. Thanks for coming to class. Did it take too long to put on your makeup?"

Stupid fucking sweater-vest poser asstroll.

The dronebots in the class all laugh. This is what he says almost every day. And it still pisses me off. I make an ape noise and the girl in front of me—Ashley—who is turned around laughing at me—gets this "I just smelled poo" look and faces front, saying, "Oh my god, some people shouldn't live. Freak."

Rhinefart turns and writes something on the board, and I block out all the conversation around me. Peace. I find a folded up piece of paper stuck in my book and take a chewed up pencil out of my pocket. I chew on the pencil some more. Wood tastes good. That thought repeats like a vinyl track skipping. Wood tastes good wood tastes good wood tastes good.

Maybe I'll draw a clown? A scary clown. Like these people are. I hear a conversation behind me about some lame bonfire tonight. I wonder what Gretch and I should do tonight. Maybe I can talk her into the two-backed beast—it's been a while. Like a looooong while. Damn I love that beast. Her place. Mom gone. Gates of heaven. And then a movie or something. A cuddle. It's the only time I can get my Gretch to schnoogs with me. Otherwise, she goes porcupine.

Tonight.

Wood tastes good.

Shit. Tonight.

Dread spreads through me. After school I'll have to take off the nail polish right away. And the eyeliner. What time is that thing at? I shoot a look back to Rachel, this totally repressed chick who wears long sleeves and long skirts all the time. Rachel would know the time. She looks up and catches my eye and I look away real fast. I don't think she knows me. I don't think. Not like this, anyway.

I realize I've been scratching at the paper in front of me and the pencil's broken through and is writing on the desk. Ashley has turned around again and she sees the pencil marks.

She rolls her eyes. "Jesus, Dylan. Can you have your psychotic break in a different class? Like, when you're not sitting by me?" She's so hot. And such a bitch. She flips around and her hair wafts strawberries at me. How is it bitchy people smell so good? Totally unfair.

She said Dylan. She knew my name.

Sweet.

Rhinefart is babbling about fucking cosine this and fucking sine that. He tries his best to fit into the football coach/math teacher stereotype. He's awesome at it.

As he is telling "the girls" some measuring cup metaphor that's supposed to relate to trig, some dudette peeks through the door. She works in the office and I see her everywhere. She's chirpy.

Chirp chirp, "Mr. Rhinehart! Sorry to bother you."

Rhinefart looks annoyed. "Yeah?"

She skips in and says, "The office says I'm supposed to give this announcement." She clears her throat and her eyes get wider. "We will be passing around a sheet today to sign up for the Boulder House senior trip." She hands a paper to Rhinefart, then bounces out of the room. Rhinefart stares at her ass. He's classy that way.

I should get Gretch to go. Field trip = different places for us to do it. Plus, a day NOT at this torture chamber called high school. I'll put our names on the sheet when it comes along. She'll never agree to it, so I'll have to forge her name. Wouldn't be the first time. After an hour of throwing words at me like "patriarchy" and "death by hot poker" she'll forgive me. I mean, it's been four years and she hasn't dumped me yet.

Rhinefart drones on. I draw a picture of a scary clown. He looks a lot like Rhinefart. I make the clown fart. There. Portrait done. I should charge him.

The sheet comes to me and I write my name on it, then write Gretch's. Boulder House is mad sick and I know Gretch will like it. After she kills me.

I pass the sheet to Ashley, totally expecting her to pass it up. But holy balls, oh, damn, oh what have I done, she actually signs it. I'm going to be in so much trouble. Like. So much trouble. Jesus help me. Ashley is basically Gretch's arch nemesis. And I just stuck them on a bus together. Wuh-oops.

And then the bell rings.

I still have to make it through the day. I don't know what is worse—having to stay at this fucking school and get thrown into a locker every five minutes or do the thing tonight.

The thing tonight. Definitely. I'm faking it there. But I don't want to hurt my parents' feelings.

Later, when I have actually made it through the day and have been knocked into a locker like six more times and the last bell rings, I sprint out of school without even saying bye to Gretch. Which makes a shitty day even shittier. But I can't be late.

I duck behind the dumpsters.

Take off the nail polish.

Put on the khakis, white shirt, loafers.

Part hair on side. Comb over. Smooth down.

Scrub off the black eyeliner.

Pray that no one sees me.

Jump on my bike and pedal like the wind home. Back to prison. I can feel everything cool slide off of me the closer I get. Transformation to dronebot complete when I ride my bike across my huge-ass lawn. Every blade is flawless, chemically enhanced. Greener than grass should be. All for show. I open the garage and park my bike in the spot where it goes and smooth down my pants. Pat down my hair. Mom meets me at the door to our huge three-story McMansion piece of shit. Her long skirt brushes her ankles. "You're late, young man. But grab a cookie before you change and get crumbs on your good outfit. "

She grabs my collar, straightens it out, and brushes imaginary lint and crap off the front of my shirt.

I flinch, half-swat her hands away from me, hoping she doesn't notice the folds in my shirt from being in my bag. I take a huge bite of the cookie. "Thanks, Mom," I say, chewing. And then I swallow and paste on an angelic smile. "I can't wait for tonight."

ASHLEY

I so want to go to private school. The people in this school are such losers.

But daddy-o sure wouldn't like it. Bad for the old campaign. Soon-to-be Senator Garrett couldn't brag about being a hometown boy.

Whatever.

I get out of my Lexus and walk to the shit-yellow school building I have to endure for the rest of the year. Then it's California, Stanford, law school, life. Out of this shithole town.

But in the meantime, I gotta play the game.

Without meaning to, I look for Gretchen's trash car, bright orange and rusted. The thing sounds like a jet engine and smells as bad. I make myself stop looking for it and stare straight ahead. She's nothing. Less than nothing. Not worth my time.

I swing my hair, stare down a freshman who's staring at me, and click-clack my way to the front door. I see that freak Dylan—Gretchen's boyfriend—pop up behind a dumpster and hurry in the front doors before me. Jesus. Of course he hangs out behind a dumpster.

Kaleigh, Jane, and Madison are waiting on the other side of the front doors. I don't even look at them when I come in, but they follow behind me anyway. We are such a '90s teen movie, it's like we're playing pretend. Seriously. But know what? It works. I know what to expect from people, and they know what to expect from me. Better to be on top than to have nuance. Nuance is for losers.

"Are we going to the bonfire tonight?" Jane says from behind me, voice all hopeful. She's the spazzy one, way too eager to please. But she works in the counseling office and is useful for hall passes.

I roll my eyes. "Yeah. Because what's really fun is dry-humping on a cornstalk in forty-degree weather."

Next to me, Kaleigh and Madison share a mean smile.

Madison says, "So, what are we doing tonight, then?" Her legs look awesome in her skirt. I make myself totally ignore them.

"Duh," I say. "What else are we going to do? We live in Wisconsin. It's pretty much the bonfire or die of boredom."

At my locker, I twirl the combination and open the door in three swift moves. The small mirror shows the three girls behind me. I check everything: lipstick—good. Eyeliner—not smudged. Hair—perfect. I grab my books and slam the door shut.

Then I see Paul down the hall. If *he's* going tonight, he'd make it interesting. He's been an interesting twist this year. New, from California—like, *cool* Cali, Berkeley, I hear. Uber liberal, I'm sure. But I could look past that, especially since it would irritate the shit out of my dad.

I say, "Later." Translation: *Girls, you're dismissed.*

Madison and Kaleigh take the cue and leave right away, but Jane stays put. She's smiling at me, eyes bright and way too perky.

"What?" I say, as snotty as I can.

Now she gets it. She shakes her head and runs away.

All right, Paul, here I come. I slink up to his locker. Trent and his stupid ball are just leaving. Overcompensate much, Trent?

I lean against the lockers, letting my boob touch his arm. "Coming to the bonfire tonight?" I'm pretty sure he gets a boner. Guys are so fucking easy.

He lowers his eyelids like he's stoned and says, "Depends on if you're going." He smiles. Clearly he thinks he's sexy but I smell dork on him like it's cologne. Whatever. He'll do.

I shrug and bat my eyelashes. For real. It works. "Maybe." I walk away, making sure I move my ass back and forth.

Putty. He's putty in my hands.

The halls are mostly empty now but everyone gets out of my way as I walk. Except for Gretchen.

Gretchen. A zip of adrenaline puts her in clearer focus. My stomach suddenly has butterflies and this irritates me. I hide a smile.

I hate Gretchen. In theory. I have to, really. We were born to hate each other—we are exact opposites. She's a social justice warrior idiot—a *poor* social justice warrior idiot, which means she's, like, not smart enough to dig herself out of the trailer-trash hole she's in. At least that's what my dad says about poor people in private, when he's not campaigning, and when he conveniently forgets that our money was inherited. Anyway, she refuses to be a part of mainstream society. With her stupid bleach-blonde hair (looking perfect around her face, with her gray-green eyes and her dark, perfect eyebrows) . . . no makeup (but awesome skin) . . . bizarro outfits (that somehow work and make her look like a badass. With awesome curves) . . . She's just weird. And artsy. I hate artsy. It's not real life. High school is survival of the fittest. And she *chooses* to go extinct.

But. She is the only one in this school—and I mean THE only one—who can match me. The only one who even tries. If I didn't officially hate her, I'd think this feeling to see her is excitement. My stomach tightens as I get near her and my skin starts to tingle.

When I get close, I'm delighted to see that her outfit is going to be easy to make fun of today. Sometimes I have to stretch, but today will be easy.

She stands in front of me and I give her the up and down.

"Gretchen! I see you've embraced your Sasquatch roots." She's wearing faux fur—faux because she's a hippie vegan I'm sure—everywhere. Even on her leg warmers.

She smiles sweetly. "Ashley. Don't you have some children to deport? Or gay people to burn? Or sulfur to roll in?"

The skin tingle turns to a cold sweat. Holy shit. I smile back and give a fake laugh, but that's all I can muster. She can't possibly know . . . but damn. She hit a little too close to home.

I walk around her and make sure I look like I smelled

something disgusting and then hurry up to Rhinehart's class, shaking the whole exchange off. No time for these stupid, bizarre feelings around Gretchen Mavis, of all people. I swallow everything down and walk through the door to Rhinehart's class. He's a dick but he gives me an A, either because he thinks I'm hot or because he's scared of my dad. Or both.

By the time I sit down in class, I've willed my heartrate back to normal. I flip my hair back and cross my legs. Swallow everything down and come back to reality. Rhinehart smiles at me and doesn't even try to look anywhere but my cootch. The guy is so gross I could hurl. And then Gretchen's freak boyfriend (why is she with him? why??) slips in behind me and Rhinehart's eyes are off me. Thank God. I flip around and say something—I don't even know what—to Dylan, just to keep him in his place. My voice still has an edge to it and I'm meaner than normal to him. I feel a little bad but push that down, too. And then Jane bounces into the room from the counselor's office to announce a field trip to Boulder House. She tries to catch my eye but I ignore her.

I need a distraction. Something fun. And Boulder House? My mind has started working, big time.

So, on any given day, a field trip to anything would make me break out into hives, especially to something as stupid as the Boulder House. But an idea has formed and the thought is so damn delicious I actually have to squirm in my chair, I'm so turned on.

Tonight when I go home, I'll find a Plunder "friend" and see if we can rendezvous there. Field trip, people around, public place . . . So risky. Which makes it ridiculously hot. I cross my legs again and squeeze. Yum. Gretchen's stupid face flashes in my head. I need her out of there, out of my head. So I conjure up my last Plunder hookup and get lost thinking about the thrill of the whole thing.

I smile and bite my pen. Totally signing up for the shithole field trip. I'll make the girls go, too, just for some added excitement.

As I sign the paper, it's like Gretchen is a figment of my imagination.

GRETCHEN

School can suck my ova.

My last class of the day and it's my worst one. Ms. Olson is droning on about capitalism. True to form, like everyone else in this goddamn town, she's ignorantly dry-humping the American dream like it actually exists.

The kicker: she starts going off on affirmative action.

I raise my hand.

She looks at my hand, sighs, and ignores me.

I put my hand down and start talking anyway. "I mean, if things were a level playing field, then maybe capitalism would work. But we don't exactly have that, do we? So we need affirmative action. Studies have shown that people hire others who are like them. So if every person who does the hiring is a rich white guy, guess who they're going to hire?"

She rolls her eyes. My teacher actually rolls her eyes at me.

Ashley turns around with a glare. I glare right back. Then she faces forward and sticks her manicured hand in the air.

Ms. Olson says, sweet-like, "Yes, Ashley?"

"Well, my dad, who is running to be a senator, says that affirmative action is taking away jobs from good, hardworking Americans—"

"You mean white guys who get things handed to them," I interrupt.

A few kids snicker.

With a glance over her shoulder, Ashley goes on, "I mean

GOOD, hardworking Americans. Affirmative action is sort of like reverse racism."

She smiles at me. Her awful wolf smile. It should make her ugly, but it doesn't. Does she believe her father's bullshit? Or even her own?

But before I can lunge at her, the bell rings. Ms. Olson calls over the loud shuffling of students packing up and heading to the door, "Last chance to sign up for the Boulder House field trip, seniors! And remember, if you're signed up, you're committed. You miss it, you have to take finals! If you don't go, you just have study hall that day. The paper is on my desk."

Right. Like I'd ever in a million years go on a field trip with this school of fuckwits. Or as Dylan says, asstrolls. Or dronebots. He's got a lot of names for them; it helps him cope, at least. Honestly Dylan needs all the help he can get. I feel that restless feeling well up in me again. It makes me mean. But, as much as I love Dylan, I need something . . . different.

I look up and Ashley gives me a fake sweet smile and I flip her off. Then I grab my monster bag and get out of the room fast, my fur boots knocking against each other. The hall is full of people running to their lockers.

I look around for Dylan but he's nowhere to be seen, which is weird because he's normally all over me. I'm a little relieved—I end up having to defend that boy *all the time.* He constantly needs to be taken care of. Like a little brother. And today I'm just so tired. Which reminds me, Mom's shift is over at 7:00 so I should start dinner around 6:00. Which leaves me enough time to run to Goodwill and find some clothes to tear up and repurpose.

I feel myself relax.

I think of a project. If I can find a skirt and then some scraps to make an applique of a girl throwing up, put on button eyes . . . Wear it during civics class with Ms. Olson, who wants to fail me so bad she can taste it but can't justify it because I am articulate and follow directions. This is going to kick ass. I can wear it tomorrow.

I walk to my gigantic '90s Buick—Michelle—who is on her last leg, and I can feel the snickers from people around me. They're laughing at Michelle, but I honestly don't care—she's everything to me. They were probably given cars from their grandparents or had to pay, like, payments to their rich parents who are teaching them to be "responsible." Fuck that. I had to beg, borrow, and . . . whatever. I worked hard for Michelle. She's freedom. She's beautiful. She's mine. She's everything I want out of a partner in crime.

Plus, she's a better companion than Dylan, if I'm honest. She's sassy, interesting, and . . . If I could only figure out how to let Dylan go.

I hear someone say, "Nice boots," so I flip them off and climb into my girl. I know I look way better than these idiots at the school do any day. And when I'm the youngest contestant to win Project Runway—I'll be making my audition tape this summer— guess who will be laughing last? Which reminds me, I should look for fabric at Goodwill I can use to make Mom a dress. She deserves one. And she'll need it for New York fashion week.

I decide to stop home before Goodwill so I can drop off my bag, but when I get there I'm surprised to see my mom's car.

Shit. She's probably got stomach problems again.

Walking into the back door of our Section 8 duplex, I yell, "Mom?"

Her small voice says, "In here honey."

She's sitting at the Formica kitchen table, working on a cross-word puzzle. Her face is pale, paler than usual.

I sit across from her and she looks up and smiles. Her eyes crinkle in the kindest way when she smiles. She's the type of person that people just automatically talk to, because they can tell she's just good.

People never just talk to me, which is fine. I take after my dad. Except in that one way where I don't abandon my family.

I can feel my forehead crease. "Stomach again?"

She puts her hand on mine. "Not too bad. But enough so that I had to cut the shift short."

I stand up and shake my head. "You have to quit eating processed shit, Mom. Your Crohn's can't take it."

I unload the grocery bags I see on the counter. Ramen noodles. Macaroni and cheese. Instant Mashed Potatoes. Cheap meals. All crap that will make her feel awful . . .

I flip around. "I'm going to Goodwill tonight, so I'll come back with something good." I rummage around in the refrigerator until I find veggies just on the point of turning and then find some bouillon back in the cupboard. We'll have good soup tonight. And I can make bread. My mood cheers.

My mom smiles at me and I smile back. She says, "You are the light of my life, you know that, don't you?"

I smile back but turn around quickly. It's a dark fucking world if I'm the light.

WHEN MAXWELL CARTWRIGHT JR. CUT into the boulder to build the House, they say a murder of crows landed and perched in the trees around him. They stayed there until they starved to death, every last one of them. The forest floor turned black with their corpses.

Every day, Maxwell dug deep into the cursed land, forming the House so that it wrapped itself around and above and in and through the boulder. Until the House was the land and the land was the House.

He hired vagrants and wanderers, people easily forgotten, to labor and hack and cut and sweat until the foundation of the House took form. They say those unfortunate workers sacrificed unwillingly—their bones becoming the very foundation of the House—so that Maxwell's power grew unchecked.

When the last stone of the House in the boulder was laid, Maxwell looked at what he had wrought and rolled his shoulders. He cracked his neck. He smiled a wicked smile. Lightning struck each tree that stood around him. The wind, starting as a breeze, blew with a gale force so fierce it blew the bones of the crows three counties over. They say the land glowed red. Some say his eyes did, too.

But he wasn't finished. Maxwell Cartwright Jr. had just begun.

He started collecting. He traveled to the farthest corners of the Earth, bringing back enchanted and cursed objects, objects that seemed to have a life of their own. Anything and everything and everyone that caught his eye, he bought, he stole, he bartered for. But his favorite way of procuring his collection was to play for it. Maxwell Cartwright Jr. loved to play games. Because he always won.

He added warehouse upon warehouse to his creation, rooms to house his collections as he won them. Rooms that ran one into another so that those who entered were enveloped completely, stuck in the twisting paths of his twisted mind. He gave these rooms themes, sinister homes for the objects he now owned. Maxwell added bands that played by themselves, fortunetellers in glass cases. He recreated entire streets stuck in time, built huge scenes with mythical creatures. He collected snow globes and sailboats, sculptures and statues, mannequins and marionettes. He built a carousel—fierce and fulsome—collecting and procuring creature after creature to ride, each more fearsome than the last. And always, always he collected dolls, old and tattered and legion. The result was a House not sane, that held within it a seething energy. Maxwell's seething energy. Of games played and lost, and evil seen and succumbed to. With each object he won, his soul went further into the darkness, his obsession twisting in on itself like a coiled snake.

After years of building and hauling and placing, of collecting and plotting and devising and playing, Maxwell Cartwright Jr. finished the last warehouse and surveyed his creation as a whole.

Now his precious collection had its place. A place to sit and seethe.

Waiting for the next poor souls to join them.

Excerpt from pp. 45-47, *The Collections of Maxwell Cartwright Jr.*

VIOLET

Paul is standing right next to me and I can smell him. He's beautiful. I am sweating.

Ms. Harper has allowed us to wander through the Maxwell Cartwright Jr. Information Center before the actual House tour starts. Even the information center—the thing that's supposed to give you a sense for what you're getting into—is filled with tons of random things.

I've been here before with my family, but I was totally scared. I think I cried the whole time. I'm still freaked out by this place, truth be told. There are, like, 30 rooms and they're all full of crazy things. Everything is dark and dusty and random; the entire house is a weird collection of weird collections.

But none of that matters right now because somehow, Paul has ended up looking at a ledger with me. It's there in front of us, inside a glass case. I can't move. I can only smell him.

Beautiful. Paul.

He laughs a little, then points to the ledger. Weather patterns, strange symbols, money to the penny, hours to the second, are written down in artistic strokes.

"Anal," Paul says.

I laugh too loud. I snort, actually. A snot bubble comes out of my nose. Oh, dear god, please tell me he didn't see that.

I swallow and say, "Yeah. It's . . ." He looks at me and I swallow again. "Anal." I finish.

He looks disappointed. Probably because he didn't know that I AM THE MAYOR OF STUPIDTOWN.

I clear my throat and say, "So weird, because the ledger is anal, but the rest of the House seems crazy chaotic. Like, how did he keep track of all this freaky stuff?"

Paul's beautiful eyes brighten. "For real, right? Have you been here before?"

We are having a conversation we are having a conversation we are having a conversation.

I force a nod. "Just once, when I was little. Have you?"

He shakes his head. "No. We just moved this year from California."

Oh, Paul. I know you did. I know everything about you.

"Really?" I say. "Do you miss it?" And then I add, "From where in California?" Like I don't know he's from San Francisco and his mother used to teach at Berkeley. Because my mother and his mother both work at UW now and I made her find out everything about his mom and him that she could.

I am thorough. That's how I get good grades. I am most certainly not a stalker. My cell phone vibrates yet again. Speaking of stalkers.

Paul is talking: "San Francisco, actually. My mom used to teach at Berkeley. And yeah, I miss it. But I'm looking forward to snow. Snow is cool . . ."

His voice is silky. He sounds different than when I accidentally go out of my way to eavesdrop on him at school. He sounds like he's comfortable right now or something. Hope flashes through me. I look at his nice, brown eyes. He seems like a really good, beautiful, incredibly hot person. Maybe he wouldn't be grossed out by me and what I've done. But then I feel my face get red.

Of course he would. *I'm* grossed out by what I've done. Am doing.

Ashley sidles up behind him and leans into him. "Paul, thank god you're on this trip. You're the only person here who's worthwhile." She flips her hair.

I'm standing here, right?

Paul looks at me and she follows his gaze and looks me up and down. She says, "Who is this?"

I open my mouth, then close it. She goes on. "Anyway, I brought this flask and I am totally ready to get the fuck out of here, so do you want to follow me? Let's start this tour early. I am NOT going with the rest of these peasants, I'll tell you that. Especially not with that freak Gretchen." She blinks her gorgeous blue eyes and licks her lips.

Paul looks at me again and then half-closes his eyes at her—maybe he's sleepy? "I don't know, it might be cool if we expand this party."

She says, "She can come, too. Whatever. Bring who you want."

And then she turns on her really high heel and walks toward the entrance of the House.

Paul made sure I would come. Who cares that Ashley Garrett doesn't know who I am? Or if she does, thinks I'm literal poop? Paul asked *me*, literal poop, to come.

I look around and see Ms. Harper talking to some other students. She's gesturing in huge movements—she's one of those poor excited teachers who likes her job. I feel sorry for her. But it looks like we could actually make it out of the entrance without her knowing.

Paul edges toward the entrance and Ashley, then turns and smiles at me. He flicks his head in a "come on, this way" gesture. It's the cutest thing I've ever seen. Warmth spreads all the way through me. Normally I would never disobey a teacher or do anything naughty. Except for that one really big thing—nothing like this. But this is Paul. And he is reaching out his hand to me.

I reach out and take his hand and we smile at each other.

The warmth shoots through me now. I can't stop smiling.

"Wanna go through this crazy chaotic House with me?"

I nod and he looks at my mouth for a second and leans in, and my body turns liquid. Lightning flashes in my down there parts. Is he . . . is he going to kiss me?

Do, Paul, do. I know we barely know each other, but I have crushed on you forever. Go ahead. I want to.

I WANT TO.

But then he snaps his head back when he hears Gretchen and Dylan move up behind us. He leans back and in the voice he uses in school, says, "Cool. Let's do it, then."

GRETCHEN

Dylan won't stop giving me his "I'm sorry" puppy eyes. Which really means he's just sorry we didn't do it on the bus, which is just logistically stupid anyway. But I know he thinks he can talk me into doing it some place in the House. Truth be told, it's been a while since I've wanted to do it with him anywhere. Maybe a change of venue is the thing. He's just not . . . what I want right now. But that's something I don't think about because I have no time for the drama that will definitely come up if we have to talk about it.

But still, the little weasel can't just sign me up for shit. It's the principle of the matter.

Unlike everyone else on this damn trip, though, I've never been to Boulder House. We never took *Leave It to Beaver* vacations like this when I was growing up. My dad left way too early for vacations. Everyone else is only here to get out of school, but I have to admit: I am actually, totally, 100 percent digging this place. This is completely my type of place. It's so funky, I can hardly stand it. And we're just in the information center. I want to live here.

Not that I'd let Dylan know.

He stares at me again with his cloudy baby blues, cloudy like a storm coming in, and looks up through his eyeliner. The boy is good-looking in a faux tweaked-out heroin sort of way. I bet a ton of people must think he's actually on heroin because he's so nuts, but the only thing he's ever done is weed. We've been together since 8th grade and there's nothing we don't know about each other. Which, in some ways, sucks.

Dylan tugs on my pinkie and motions toward the entrance to the House. Ashley, Paul, and that quiet girl (Vicky?) are looking around all stupid like no one can see them. Actually Ms. Harper can't, and everyone else seems to be texting.

Dylan whispers, "Let's blow this bitch, baby. Go through the House in our own time. I'll make it up to you for dragging you along, I promise. And I think this is your kinda place, for realsies."

I stare daggers at him. "So now you want to add detention to the list of shit you're putting me through." I don't even try to keep my voice down and Ms. Harper half looks up then keeps talking, waving her arms around so she looks like she's batting away flies.

He looks away and swallows, then looks back. "Baby . . ."

I sigh like I'm doing him the biggest favor in the world. But I'm already designing a new clothing line based on this place. I'm getting that itchy feeling I get when I want to start sketching. I pat the pocket of my monster bag to make sure I've got my sketchbook. There's the outline of a magazine in there, too—something I brought along just for eye candy. There's a girl in the mag I think is stupid hot. My girl-on-girl fantasies have been on point lately. I shoot a look at Dylan. I wish I could fantasize about him and still get off. I wish I wanted to have sex with him again. I just . . . don't. For, like, a year now.

I say to him, "Fine. Let's go. But you owe me big time."

Dylan smiles like a maniac and crosses his eyes then gives this weird half-assed gang sign he made up and always does and will probably get shot for someday. His black fingernails flash and I can't help but give a half-smile. The boy is seriously weird. I adore him, even if I don't want to do him.

I look toward the entrance again and watch Ashley, Paul, and the girl disappear, then I wait a few beats. No way am I running into Ashley Garrett in there, the bitch-hole. I never use that word lightly, either—sister strength and all that. But Ashley Garrett is pure-D bitchitude and a traitor to our sex, so she gets zero respect from me.

I look at Dylan sideways and he smiles and inches away from the group of students. I inch away, too, and for once, for whatever reason, no one notices us go. Which is weird because everyone is always noticing me.

We show our tickets to the bored attendant in front of the entrance to the House. I peek around the corner, excitement shooting through me like a first kiss. This is going to kick ass.

PAUL

I would not wish any companion in the world but you.

God help me, but Shakespeare quotes—this one from *The Tempest*, stormy like how my hormones are right now—are running through my head. It's hard to think when her pretty face is taking up all the space. I'm half-swaggering, half-skipping. I forget how I'm supposed to walk.

Violet is pretty, for sure, but there's something else. Something sweet and smart and . . . something that makes me want to put capes on mud puddles and be all chivalrous and stuff. She, like, listens when I talk. And isn't fronting AT ALL. For real. I know this because she always does something kind of awkward around me. It's adorable. Like she always accidentally snorts when she laughs and then goes bright red. Which I'm pretty sure means she likes me back. I mean, she's like the least secretive person I've ever met. My mom would say, "She has no guile." Plus, she's soft.

I put my hand on the small of her back as we move toward the entrance to the actual House in the boulder. Ashley's high heels flash before us.

The entrance is actually up this long, bridge-like ramp that zigzags up to the House. The layout of this place is mad bizarre. All of it. You drive through the parking lot and there are these HUGE sculptures with gigantic metal bugs and worms and stuff on them. So . . . great mood killer there. Then you go into the lodge-like building that looks like it's the only building but it's actually just sitting on one hill. Then, in the back of the lodge you go up the ramp we're going up now to get to the House that sits on an adjacent hill to the right. Then you have to go back down the ramp to the lodge where the entrance to the warehouses is. It's like a fever dream or something. I'm already disoriented and I've just started the tour. I caught a glimpse of the warehouses when I was walking into the lodge. I could see buildings climbing down the hill to the left, going down, down, down, like they were part of the landscape. So far downhill that the shadow of the House covers them.

Ashley turns around like she's reading my mind. "The House is fine, but it's the warehouses we should go to. The House is too small to get lost in." She winks at me and half-scowls at Violet, like she can't even muster the energy to dislike her.

My kingdom for a horse to run Ashley over. If I had a sword . . . I probably wouldn't do anything, if I'm honest. But I'd want to. For Violet.

We reach the top of the ramp where an old-fashioned looking sign says, THIS WAY FOR THE TOUR. The three of us stop and look at it. I feel Violet stiffen next to me and I wonder if she's actually scared. I have to admit, the sign is . . . well, strangely terrifying. The letters are written in a font that I'd imagine the devil might use on the contract to buy your soul.

Ashley turns and says to me, "Well, here we go. Into the mouth of the beast." Something flashes across her face, but then she winks and turns on her super high heel and goes through the door.

Now, I am not a person who believes in ghosts or the supernatural or anything. Like, I tried for years to feel or hear or see something from my dad that said he forgave me and nothing—I mean NOTHING—happened. But if I did believe in that stuff, I would swear there is a shimmer when Ashley walks through the entrance. It freaks me out, so without even thinking, I grab Violet's hand.

She stares at our hands and stays still. I am barely breathing. I think about how ballsy this move was, accident or not, and suddenly I lose my nerve, so I let go.

Why'd I let go?

Violet smiles at me, and I feel a loosening up of everything in her. Which makes me stand up taller.

We lock eyes, and she gives me a little head movement that says, "Let's go." The same one I gave her to get her to sneak away with me. Goddamn it's adorable. I take a look at the sign again and another Shakespeare quote pops into my head, this time from *Macbeth*: "Tis the eye of childhood that fears a painted devil."

Just a painted devil, that sign. The eerie feeling clamped on my nervous system? Just a superstitious fantasy. And anyway, about right now, I'd travel to hell and back for Violet.

This time I mean to grab her hand. And I don't think twice when together we walk through the door, side-by-side.

DYLAN

Gretchen peek-a-boos me from the corner of her eye. I know this look—she is trying to be mad still but isn't feeling it. Hopefully her look also means she's horny. Adrenaline spikes through me and I feel that fire of turn-on. Yeehaw. I love me some Gretch when she's horny. Which lately hasn't been, like, ever. I shift my legs and try to let my down-theres breathe. We go through the entrance to the ramp thingy that leads all the way up to the door.

"You haven't been here, right?"

I snort. "As if."

Gretchen nods, her eyebrows furrowed. "Yeah, some of us don't get vacations. We're too busy trying to, you know, pay for heat."

"Yeah," I say, and swallow a big ol' glob o' guilt down. Gretch thinks my family is, um, different than what it is? I may have told her that my parents were never around. And poor. And might have hinted that they were neglectful. Truth is, I have been here before. My parents took me here like five years ago. They thought Satan built this place. They might be right. A lesson and a warning and a weekend outing all wrapped up in one creepy visit. I guess families are supposed to do that shit. The outing part anyway.

She moves on. "Look at these statues." She points to some skeletons, at their blank eyeholes. "And remember those ones we saw coming in with the things crawling on them?" Her own eyes are bright. She is digging this place.

I mush my lips into her neck, pushing her until she hits the side of the ramp.

She pushes me off. "Jesus, Dylan."

But I felt her curves in the shuffle and my body is starting to heat up.

Too bad we're at the entrance now. But . . . it's, like, there's something covering the doorway, kind of like a film. Hard to see, but if you look just right . . . Jell-O-y. Like if I stuck my hand in the doorway, goo would slather my arm and turn me into a goo-monster. I don't remember that from last time. I look at Gretch and then turn back to the entrance. The Jell-O has vanished. Did I imagine it?

Gretch doesn't hesitate—something I love about my girl—and we walk straight in. It takes a minute for my eyes to adjust and I swear when I hear the door shut, it sounds final. Like an Amen. If I was a Catholic, I'd give the sign of the cross.

"Whoa," she whispers.

I breathe in her ear, "Wait till you get to the warehouses."

She flips her head to me. "I thought you hadn't been here before."

I feel the oops-blood rush to my head. Nice one, Dylan. I stutter. I stammer. I swallow. And then I come up with this: "I heard Ms. Harper say it."

Her eyes narrow and I know she doesn't believe me. So I do what I would do with my mom and dad when I want the heat off. I point randomly.

The best thing about pointing anywhere in the Boulder House is you are guaranteed to land on something rad.

I end up pointing at a stained glass coffee table in another room. And it is mega-cool. It's some samurai dragon shit or something. It's long and big and takes up the entire room. We walk to the room and lean in, looking at the table. It's got people-shaped shapes in some of the panes in the table. Looks like they're screaming—it's creepy with a capital DAMN.

"What *is* this place?" she wonders out loud.

We move past the table, down the stairs. Tan carpet worn from thousands of feet trampling grosses up the House, but otherwise it is a motherfucking house in a motherfucking boulder. It's dark and gloomy—swirly dust dances around us every time we move. You have to duck to get around things. There are swank '70s corners with velvet couches that you just KNOW Max-Whatever used for some love shacking. There's also a kitchen and a ginormous fireplace that is actually fire-placing with actual fire. Like, *crackling*. Little windows here and there shoot out shafts of light. But it's a losing battle. The place is shadow and dust.

I feel like something's missing, but I don't know what it is.

Gretchen has stopped to look at a cubbyhole with a baby grand piano.

It bursts out playing and Gretchen screeches and jumps.

Hell, I jump, too. Then I remember, this place is full of instruments that play by themselves. Fucked. Up. And awesome.

I put my man-child arms around Gretchen and she half leans into me, half feels ready to pounce. That about sums up our relationship.

She flips around and her hair is gleaming from some light up and behind her. She looks like an angel. My heart falls in love with her just a little more.

"This place is so freaky." She smiles big. "I love it!" I can't help but smile big, back.

"Yeah, it's pretty rocking. Like you." I lean in to kiss her, but she's already gone. We've walked through the whole part of the House that is in the boulder and we've already hit the eternity room.

My dad wouldn't go out there the last time we came—the huge, all-glass room perched on the boulder. There are tons of mirrors in there, so you see yourself and the landscape all around over and over and over, stretching off to infinity. But the bottom is clear. The room sticks out, like 200 feet up, over the forest, so you're constantly aware of the distance to the ground. Thinking about what it would be like to fall. Or what it would be like to walk on air.

My dad said, "If God wanted us to walk on air, he'd have given us winged feet."

My mom laughed hard at that one. You know. God humor.

Now, as Gretch and I stand at the big entrance to the room, with another self-playing band starting up—this time with the theme from *Jaws*, nice touch—I realize what's been poking at my brain.

People.

Or, like, their absence.

There's no one in here.

Uneasiness starbursts on my skin, prickle prickle. Maybe it's because it's in the middle of the day. Maybe they cleared it out for the school trip?

The starbursts turn to sweat. Something ain't right.

Gretch has walked into the eternity room and is staring down to the trees below. "Holy shit, Dylan. This place is INSANE!"

Her words seem to echo off the glass. And right at that moment, the *Jaws* theme stops. I hear the ticking of the clock somewhere. And then *it* stops.

Just, silence. A bead of sweat trickles down my temple. "Gretch, babe, let's go see those freaky warehouses Ms. Harper was talking about."

She takes one last long look at the forest floor way below, then up at herself and the forest around us, and walks to me. I am looking around me, eyes darting everywhere. When she gets to me, she and all the other Gretchens in the mirror say, "What's up, squirrely?"

"Where are Paul and Ashley? And that other girl, Violet?"

Gretchen shrugs and furrows her eyebrows. She always looks mean when she does that, but she's actually not pissed. It still scares people off. I think she likes it. "Who gives a shit?"

I nod. "Yeah. I guess."

Her eyes shine into mine and the clouds break up. She says, "I have about eight ideas for a line of clothing." She hooks her arm through mine and we get out of the boulder part of the House, go down another ramp, and stand at the entrance to the warehouses.

As we leave, I hear the *Jaws* music start up again.

ASHLEY

I knew Paul was a dork.

From the actual House in the actual boulder, the ramp sends us right back to the same entrance and then we are supposed to get our tickets punched for the second part of the tour, which is the weird-ass warehouses. I sashay my way to the entrance and wait for the lovebirds to follow. Here I am flirting like a fiend, for appearances, and Paul-the-dork doesn't even care. He's mooning over Madame Boring. Whatevs. I'd think it was cute if a) I had a heart, and b) it wasn't getting in the way of what I need from Paul. Which is a cover.

I read over the text messages from my Plunder hook up again: Russiandelite4. Yeah, classy name.

Russiandelite4: The bathroom of which house?

Me: Boulder House. You go to the room with the windmill outside. In the warehouses. It's the first bathroom when you go in. On the right.

Russiandelite4: what is this Boulder house?

Me: the place where we get to know each other REAL well 😈

Russiandelite4: Tell me what you like . . .

Me: I like you to meet me there at 1:00 on Oct. 31. Yeah?

Russiandelite4: Yeah. I like.

Me: how about wearing the same bra from your pic? Crazy hot. You won't have it on for too long . . .

Russiandelite4: how about you wear high heels from your pic? I'll start licking from there and keep going . . .

Hot. God I can't wait.

I huff a huge sigh—where the fuck is everyone? While I tap my toe as loud as I can and cross my arms over my chest, I notice the guy who was just manning the entrance isn't there anymore. No one is anywhere. Lazy-ass mooches. Probably paid with our tax dollars, too. I can actually hear my dad say these words in my head, so I shake it like I can get him out of there.

Please never let me be my dad.

I scan the windows that look through to the ramp we just came from. I hear a scraping against stone and look up the hallway that leads back to the information center. The stone walls bend around and disappear in the dark so I can't really see anything but that's definitely where the sound came from. It sounds like someone trying to move something heavy by pushing it along stone. The scraping sounds through the room again. I roll my shoulders. I'm officially going bat-shit here with all the idiots I have to hang out with.

I shift my weight on these shoes that are already killing me and swing my purse back and forth, blowing out breath that poofs my bangs. I stare back up to the ramp at Paul and Violet walking so, so slow toward me. What is taking them so long? And where is the ticket guy?

I stop for a second and really look around. There's the hallway that leads up to the information center. The door that goes to the ramp to the house part of the House. Then the other door that leads outside to the entrance of the warehouses. There is not one person in sight. My skin prickles. I listen for Ms. Harper's voice in case she's leading the class to the first part. But I hear nothing.

I shrug. We're probably just early. And I should be counting my lucky stars Ms. Harper isn't done yapping in the info center so that we have time to get ahead, instead of freaking myself out. I hop up on the small ticket desk and circle my feet.

As I kick my feet against the desk, I have a thought: What if no one else is here? As in, what if my hookup doesn't show up?

If she doesn't show, so help me . . . Worse, if it's some ass-hole 50-year-old dude masquerading on the Interwebs for some barely legal . . .

I don't let myself even think the thought. I need this. She just needs to show. And match the picture I got. And then things will be . . . more interesting anyway.

Finally, after 400 years, Paul and Violet reach me. I am giving them my best bored look. The scraping sound echoes through the room again and then I hear a thump. It's definitely coming from the hallway.

I swallow.

"What's wrong, Ashley?" Violet's voice is high and hard to hear, like a dog whistle.

I look at Paul. "Looks like the ass-munch ticket guy isn't here. We just have to go outside to the Wheel House." My heart bangs when I even say the name of the room. My hookup better be there. I point out the windows in the opposite direction of the ramp to an ornately carved door and squat building sitting next to a huge mill wheel.

From the corner of my eye, I see the door open on the other side of the room from the ramp to the House. Gretchen and Dylan.

Paul looks at Violet, mouth down in a frown. "Shouldn't we just wait for the guy? What do you think, Violet?" His voice echoes around the room.

I scorch her with a stare. She swallows and I say, "If you guys want to wait here then, whatever. I'm going in."

Another scrape on stone echoes from down the hall and two thumps sound. I can actually feel something reverberate in the ground.

I am suddenly, totally, horribly freaked out.

Gretchen and Dylan come up to us. Gretchen says to Dylan, "Oh god. We caught up to her."

I narrow my eyes at her. She does the same at me.

This time the thumps come in succession, but like a weird heartbeat: thump-thump, thump-thump, thump-thump.

I am off the desk and starting toward the door. Though I can't see anybody, I can feel them all following me. The thumping sounds are not far behind us now. Like it's getting closer. I know I'm being crazy, but it must be the damn House. And I don't care. I want out.

I try not to sprint but end up walk/running out of the room and outside to the Wheel House door without looking back. I thought for sure Gretchen and Dylan would wait at least until I got inside to follow me, but they are right there when I turn around by the door. The thought makes me feel better, actually. I wasn't making the noise up.

There's a creak and a groan and the gigantic mill wheel next to us slowly starts moving. I didn't think it was, like, a *working* mill. I look up at it and notice the sky outside has turned completely dark. The wind, out of nowhere, whips my hair across my face. I hear crows cawing.

Paul and Violet have moved closer and I see them move their hands together until they're holding hands, all the while looking at the sky, and Gretchen has her bitch look on her face like she's telling the sky to knock it the fuck off. Dylan is staring up with one eyebrow raised. The air is charged, my hair starting to stand on end.

As I'm looking around and up at the sky, I see in the center of the courtyard a gigantic bolt of lightning shoot down to one of the metal sculptures. Sparks fly and a metal tang splits my eardrums. The air smells like burning . . . everything. Underneath the tang, the cawing gets louder.

For a split second, we all look at each other. But when the second bolt of lightning shoots down, we move as one through the door to the Wheel House.

Part 666

MAXWELL CARTWRIGHT JR. OPENED HIS creation's doors to the public for free on All Hallows' Eve, 1936. They say that a line snaked through the forest two miles long, that the desperation to see wonder and beauty during the height of the Great Depression—for free—was enough to stuff the legend and the curse deep into the closet of the community's psyche. And so, despite the stories, despite the fear that raised the hairs on the backs of their necks, and despite the murder of crows watching, always watching, the people came.

And they loved it.

For years, more and more people came to the House, even after an admission fee was added, all of them ignoring the tendril of unease, the whisper of horror that followed them through the buildings, the tingle of uncertainty as they entered the rooms. Or maybe because of it. Until at last the House over the years became a roadside attraction, a family vacation—benign, affordable. Safe. But all the while the House kept growing, kept changing, kept hissing through time, undetected.

As the House's reputation grew, the local legend dimmed until there was but a spark of its real story left. Only a few of the elders remembered the legends, but as is true for all generations, their words became an inside joke to their younger relatives, a reason to put them in the nursing home.

Still there were some people, young and old, who knew for certain the stories were true. There were some who entered the House and never came out at all.

Because Maxwell Cartwright Jr. never stopped collecting.

Excerpt from p. 101, *The Collections of Maxwell Cartwright Jr.*

VIOLET

I tangle over Paul's legs and we both fall, me on top of him. Someone falls on top of me and then I feel another thwunk and heavy pressure. The door behind us slams shut so hard my teeth rattle. I feel the weight ease a little bit and then the cold feel of air as it makes its way to my face again and bodies climb off of mine. I'm still on top of Paul.

I scramble off of him and then try to grab his elbow but wind up, somehow, lifting him by his belt like a bad kid in a 1920s silent movie. But I can't lift him up much because he's a big guy so I just make an A-frame with his body, almost like he's doing a really awkward version of a yoga position.

Luckily, he's quick, so he bounds up and says, "Cool, cool," to no one, and I back up and step on Ashley's foot.

"Bitch!" Ashley pushes me forward. Paul catches me and I see him staring at her hard. He looks like he's struggling to say something.

But then Dylan says, "Uh, Three Stooges, this door is, like, closed behind us in a major way."

Gretchen feels around the edges saying, "shit shit shit" and Dylan keeps tugging at the handle.

Paul lets go of me and strides to the door. He looks cute and determined. He's so . . . stride-y. I smile for a second but when he gets there and pulls the handle with all his might, my smile disappears.

"We're stuck in here?" My voice is so high some dog

somewhere just lifted up its head. I take a look around. The room is dim and disappears into a hallway that bends around, the walls made of stone. I can't really make out anything farther down. All the carpet is velvety red, like dried blood. To my left is a gigantic fireplace and huge pots, and I can just make out a strange scene farther down the hall with knights and trees . . . Could that be right? To my right is a small window and down farther I see a sign for WOMEN'S RESTROOM. A tiny ray of light triangles on the red carpet in front of the opening.

I look out the window cut into the wall on my right and see that the mill wheel is spinning fast and the air outside is swirling. Like, clouds are funneling. Holy schmolies. I see shards of lightning strike down at intervals outside, sparks shooting with every hit. No rain. Just dark swirling air and lightning. Lightning knives.

So. Lightning knives aren't normal.

Where has love taken me?

"Guys, look outside," I say. Paul's grunting stops and so does Dylan's, and I feel everyone come stand beside me.

"Holy shit," says Ashley.

"Fuuucckkk me," says Gretchen. Ashley flips her head around to her and then looks back outside.

As if choreographed, the five of us step back from the window.

Ashley's voice is shaking. "What the holy fuck is happening? This is NOT happening. I will NOT be trapped in here!" Her last sentence verges on hysterical and she stomps a foot and her ankle turns on her heel. She stands up straight and smooths her skirt, then trains her look on Paul.

"You had better get us out of here. Try the door again!" She points a shaking finger at him.

Paul rolls his eyes. "Yeah, I'm sure it's unstuck now. And anyway, you want to go back out to that lightning storm?" He points randomly and ends up pointing at the wall. Then he casually reaches behind him and tries the door again. It is still stuck. His beautiful face falls.

Now Gretchen says to Ashley, "Good thinking, Captain Vapid."

Ashley narrows her eyes and I can tell this is going to be its own lightning storm, so I jump in fast. "Uh, wait. We've all got our phones, right? Maybe we can just call security or something?"

Ashley glares at me but doesn't say anything. Gretchen trains her eyes on me and rummages in her monster bag, "Good thinking, Vicki."

"Her name is Vi-o-let," says Ashley like she's talking to a really slow 3rd grader, and for a second I get a thrill that she knows my name and is defending me, but then I realize it's just to contradict Gretchen. Paul looks at me as he reaches in his pocket and rolls his eyes at me. I smile back. I wish his hand was still in mine.

I clear my throat and grab my phone from my pocket.

It's dead. I know I turned it on before, but no matter how many times I press the button, nothing happens.

From the look on everyone else's faces, they're in the same boat. We all look at each other and no one says anything. I put my phone away and so do Dylan, Gretchen, and Paul. The sound of lightning strikes comes through the window. And something else. I hear a squeak of iron, like a rusty hinge being opened.

Ashley shakes her phone like she can shake some power into it. She huffs again and then says suddenly, her voice still high, "I'm going to pee."

It's a good idea. I see Gretchen shrug and start moving and I begin to follow. Hate each other or not, in the history of the world, girls don't let girls pee alone.

Ashley flips around and says, "I can go alone." She glares at Gretchen.

Gretchen says, rolling her eyes, "You're not the only one who has to pee, bitchwad," and keeps walking. I don't say anything, but I have to, too. Ashley's eyes dart everywhere and I can see some sweat breaking out on her temples. She doesn't say anything but hurries in front of us.

The three of us walk down the creepy, dark hall to the light triangle. The scene to my left with the knights is so dark I can barely look in. Something in the scene flashes but when I look closer, all I see is the darkness. A knight farther down the hall is encased in glass, a light shining down on the armor, somehow making the whole thing look sinister. I look back to see Paul and Dylan standing there, not talking. Paul stares down at his shoes and then rocks back and forth from heel to toe. Dylan chews on his fingernails and bounces a leg, eyes landing and jumping off of everything, like eye parkour. I bet he does actual parkour. He seems like the type. Another squeak gets my attention and I squint down the hall.

Nothing but the knight in the glass case, lit in that eerie light.

I'm imagining squeaks. I shake my head at myself and walk into the bathroom.

Back lighting illuminates a wall of bottles of all different colors and sizes. The bathroom is made out of stone and I'm half-surprised to see the toilets aren't. I don't remember this room, but it's beautiful.

I also don't remember the House being so . . . kidnap-y.

Gretchen and I take stalls and Ashley, after peering into them and grunting like she's mad or something, looks in the mirror and reapplies her lipstick, taking a paper towel to kiss some of it off and wipe the moisture from her temples. In the mirror, I see Gretchen roll her eyes again and I kind of want to, too. I mean, come on. I thought she had to pee, but I guess she came in just to look at herself.

After doing what needs to be done, Gretchen and I come out of the stalls almost at the same time. Ashley's still primping her hair. Gretchen's lips twitch and there's some struggle on her face. Which she clearly loses because she says, "Got a hot date here in Boulder House? Jesus." She shakes her head and washes her hands.

Ashley, though, reacts like Gretchen just poked her in the boob. Her mouth works and she says after a few seconds, "No."

That's it.

We all stare at each other in a super awkward way and I'm about to say something I hope is funny because the tension is making little butterflies flutter up my spine and I want them to stop right now . . .

But then glass shatters somewhere in the hall. And the sound of little feet running makes my whole body stiffen.

A flash of something small and knee-high runs by the bathroom door.

But it's the high laugh that comes out of nowhere that makes my knees buckle.

ASHLEY

Okay, forget the fact that Gretchen is clearly a psychic witch and should probably be burned at the stake. Even forget the fact that despite the pressure I'm under by being stuck here, my hair is holding up. What I am totally freaking out about is the fact that something small and crazy-looking just ran by the fucking door.

And I could swear I saw a glimpse of hair fly by.

Boring, Witch, and I run out the door like fucking idiots TOWARD the thing. But I guess where else are we going to go? We run to Dylan and Paul who have moved farther down the hall in front of the knight in the glass case and are looking around with eyes wide and panicked. Paul's hands are out like he's trying to keep his balance on a high wire.

Dylan says, "Holy hell, Gretch, did you see something?"

Gretchen, with her bitch-brows furrowed, says, "What just ran by?"

More sounds of feet running. And now I wish I'd actually peed. A loud metal squeak echoes off the stone.

I could swear that the knight in the glass case directly across from me just moved its head. I could swear.

Okay. I've been officially driven crazy. Thanks a lot, freakoids.

Violet says, "Maybe it was a cat?"

All of us look at her and she shrinks into herself, and stammers, "I mean, what do you guys think?"

"I am so out of here," I say, but I don't move. Because no

fucking way am I going anywhere by myself. I don't know what's going on, but I want to be able to throw other people in front of me if I have to.

And then I see it.

The knight's head in the glass case moves and looks straight at me.

I'm the only one facing it. I can't talk. I can't talk. I can't even think. I just open my mouth and put my hand over it and then point.

Everyone turns around and the knight in the glass case slams his hand against the glass. The metal on glass screeches and the whole case reverberates.

Violet screams. I back up against the wall. On the other side of the knight, another knight in the space where the scene is set up takes a step forward and turns its head toward us slow, like a creepy-ass praying mantis I once saw. The rusty sound of ancient metal scraping along the walls.

Paul, looking around wildly, says, "Is this animatronic or something? Are these robots? Is this House like a haunted house or something?" His voice is shaky and he goes up an octave with every sentence like a fucking girl.

More knee-high things run past us and one knocks me over. I splat up against the wall and the thing in front of me pauses.

It stands in front of me, little mouth fixed in a smile and unblinking marble eyes taking me in.

It's a doll. A fucking doll. And it's . . . moving?

Gretchen makes a grunt sound and I look up just in time to see her kick one of the dolls. It's a small doll with a Victorian dress and it flies near me and thwumps against the wall. It gets up, stares with dead eyes at Gretchen, then runs away.

There are footsteps all around now. Little things run by us in blurs. I hear the creaking of branches and see dolls sitting in the fake trees, their gazes trained down at us. A doll's face swings down from a branch in front of me and its creepy empty eyes just stare directly in my face. And, oh, the trees seem to be real now . . . so, okay. I don't think "what the fuck is happening?" is a strong enough question.

I can only get out a squeak when something else catches my attention.

The knight in the scene has moved. No doubt about it. One more step and it's out of the dark hole where the scene is set up, over the rope, and into the hall. Where we're standing. The thing has an axe. It tries to get over the rope but can't lift its leg high enough. I turn toward the knight in the glass case. He hits the glass again; a spider-web crack blossoms around his hand.

That's enough for all of us.

Without saying a word to each other, we run. Paul first, then Violet, then me, then who gives a shit.

I can feel the whoosh of air as dolls run past me.

We round the corner of the hall and run by a storefront-looking place with glass blown out of it. Our feet start crunching glass and we all have to slow down. In the room there are other dolls. One is in a carriage, its face dirty and one eye open. It raises up one arm. The other arm gets stuck in the carriage and just falls off. This can't be real. Who do I pay to get me out of this nightmare?

No time to think about that, though: when I hear the sound of glass crashing, I run so fast, I almost knock over Paul and run over his damn body.

PAUL

It's a dream . . . It's a dream . . . To die, to sleep . . . It's just a goddamn dream.

I'mnotcrazyI'mnotcrazyI'mnotcrazy.

It has to be a joke. Someone has to be messing with us.

But I decide to run anyway. Just in case. And Violet is scared, so I should, like, try to be a man for her or something.

WHAT. THE. HELL. IS. HAPPENING?

I am in front of everyone sprinting down the hall and I want to turn around to make sure Violet is okay, but after the second sound of glass shattering I decide to assume she's back there somewhere and women are whole human beings and can take care of themselves and I wouldn't want to offend her so I run faster.

I run into the next room, which is small and mostly empty, and decide with a glance that it looks safe enough to stop. At least there are no knights or dolls or anything.

Dolls. I'm now afraid of dolls. Jesus.

Dylan brings up the rear and we are all breathing fast but the guy looks especially bad. He weighs probably 120 pounds soaking wet, but he doesn't look like he gets out much. When he clears the doorway, Gretchen finds the door—one of those pocket doors where it slides into place—and slams it shut, turning the tiny little lock.

Awesome. That will totally keep out, you know, the murderous knights after us.

I always wanted to see real knights in action. But this isn't exactly what I had in mind.

This is straight up bullshit.

That's so good I decide to say it out loud. "This is straight up bullshit!"

Ashley starts pacing and says, "I have to get out of here! I have things to do. This is not the way I'm supposed to die. This is not the way!" She is twisting her hair and every third step her ankle twists and she stumbles on her heel, but she doesn't seem to notice.

Dylan says, "Uh, dudette is losing it."

Ashley stops and turns to him. "OF COURSE I'M LOSING IT YOU TWEAKER ASSHOLE WASTE OF A HUMAN BEING!"

No one talks because Gretchen's face freezes the whole room. She steps in front of Dylan and stands face to face with Ashley. She looks like she might *bite* her. "Listen carefully, you piece of shit. You need to step off now." Gretchen's voice is low but a slight tremor travels through it. She might really kill her. Dylan says softly, "Babe . . ." I should say something, but I'm stuck to the floor. Better not to get involved.

But then something moves at the other end of the room. A mechanical click happens and a whirring sound fills the room.

I jump and Violet lets out a little shriek.

At the end of the room, a wooden box sits at eye level on a podium-like thing. Something moves in there, the same sounds clicking and whirring methodically, over and over. It's a scene. A tiny scene.

We move toward it and I look inside. It's a bedroom like in a dollhouse, but there is a sleeping guy on a bed that wakes up and then sits up, turning his head toward us, then lying back down to sleep. When he lies down, a skeleton pops out of a tiny grandfather clock, and the closet opens and a demon flies out, then back in.

This happens over and over. Click, wakes up and looks at us; click, snap, skeleton pops out of clock. Click, whir, demon flies back and forth.

Click.

Snap.

Whir.

We are all staring at the box and I feel Violet come up beside me. She lays her head lightly on my shoulder and despite the past 20 minutes, I think I might pass out from happiness. Her breath moves my sleeve, just a little bit, but I feel every brush against my skin. Click snap whir. Her breath is hot, and then my shirt is cold. Hot and then cold.

Click.

Snap.

Whir.

The sound is the only thing in the room.

Everyone's breath is slow now. No one moves.

"It's called 'The Sleeper.' A treatise on how you humans see what you want to see and close your eyes to the rest."

Violet jumps back and our group breaks up like someone rolled a bowling ball through us.

I snap my head back and to the left because that's where the voice comes from, and I see two red eyes in the corner near the pocket door. I back up into the box with the scene playing out.

Click, snap, whir.

Gretchen, her voice shaky, says, "Who *are* you?"

Violet steps forward, her big brown eyes hopeful. "Are you with the House? Can you get us out?"

Ashley takes two steps forward and jabs a finger in the direction of the voice, her purse jabbing with her, "Listen, I'm going to sue this place!"

But then the thing in the corner steps out. More like, it climbs down from the wall.

And I almost piss my pants.

The thing says, "I suppose you could say I am *with* the House." It smiles but it's like no smile I've ever seen before. And no smile I ever want to see again.

GRETCHEN

I am clutching my monster bag in front of me like it's going to protect me from whatever the holy fuck this thing is in front of me. I let go of the bag slowly and it falls on my hip.

Don't show any weakness.

The thing in front of us looks human. Like a human male. Sort of. He's wearing a really old-fashioned tuxedo; angles cut perfectly to fit his long, thin frame, his limbs so skinny they look like spider legs. Long black tailcoat, white vest, bow tie, top hat with some sort of pattern I can't make out on it. And he holds a cane. His face glows white in the dark room and his whole body stands out against the wood-paneled wall. He's sort of blurry, like he's vibrating—I can't get a beat on his exact features. He twirls his cane and then takes his top hat off and bows. His black, shiny hair doesn't move. In fact, the movement is so fast it makes me jump.

As he stands back up slow, his eyes train on me. They are red eyes. Not like bloodshot—his pupils, irises, everything are red. "What do you think of my suit, Gretchen? A little expensive for you, perhaps? Too old-fashioned? Never mind. I wanted to look sharp for our first meeting. I've been waiting for you, you see. We all have." He smiles his inhuman smile at us. His teeth are pointed, like a shark's.

I clutch the monster bag in front of me again and step back.

No one says anything. The thing in front of us twirls his cane. The whole room vibrates like a movie projector gone wrong. The scene of the guy in the bed is going faster and faster.

He takes another bow. "Welcome, you five dear souls, to my collection. And I suppose it would be rude not to thank you for coming." He looks around like he's expecting us to say something. I feel someone near my elbow and I start like an electric shock hit me, but it's just Dylan. I take a quick look around and see that the five of us have inched closer to each other. We are now one big group of fear. Ashley's perfume mixes with the musty smell of sweat and bodies.

The guy—the thing, the monster, whatever he is—starts twirling his cane again.

"We're going to play a game now, you and me." He thumps his cane on the floor and we all jump. "Though, I should warn you: the House *always* wins. And I, my dear children, am the House."

He takes a long moment to look at each one of us, fully. Something on my insides feels raw and scraped. My stomach roils, like I'm growing an instantaneous ulcer. The smell of rot and decay fills the room.

"But fear not," he adds. "Though you have no choice to play, I am not entirely without mercy. Unlike real life, you will have a chance to make it. I am not a monster, after all." A smile crawls up his face and all of us take a step back. "You are wondering about rules, yes? Indeed. For what is a game without rules?"

"What if we don't want to play?" Violet murmurs.

If he hears her, he ignores her. "My first rule is this: though I *can* take you at any time, I will not interfere. Everyone—every object, every soul—in this House makes choices here. I shall neither hinder nor help." He twirls his cane again and begins walking in a jerky, horror-movie way. "For what is a win unearned? Unsatisfying, I have found. And deeply boring. Your lives taken with no struggle . . . well. Where is the fun in that?"

He sighs. I can smell his rotting breath. Ashley makes a small, strangled sound.

"So, you have a chance, my dear Five. All is not lost for you. Yet. Your task in this game, you ask? Your task is very simple. Get out of here alive and intact. If you can do that . . ." He bows with a huge flourish. "You win." Then he straightens. "If you cannot," and now his eyes are like pits of dark, "I win. And you become mine. Part of my collection, forever."

Silence. A shudder runs through my body.

He says casually, "Any questions?"

My mind is hamster-wheeling and I can't slow it down. Finally, I swallow and say harsher than I mean to, "What does *that* mean?" Then I add because now I can't seem to stop, "How do you know my name? What game? Why us?"

Why did he mention the expensive part?

The thing smiles and starts jerking around the room again. His body streaks like a watercolor painting smearing. Like part of him has to catch up with the other part. We turn as one to watch him circle.

"I know all your names. Poor Gretchen. Jo—I mean, Dylan. Lord Paul. Ashley, the Lover. And, of course, the adventurous Violet." He winks at us and then tips his hat but keeps moving around the room. "I know what potential you have, what potential for my collection. You interest me. You are . . . complicated, yet so simple. I have no doubts you will succumb to my game." He stops suddenly and bows. "You'll fit right in here."

I feel Ashley move and hear her say, "Ew." She moves closer to the thing and says, "Listen, psycho. I don't know who you think you are, but you better let us out of here or my father—"

The thing stops fast and Ashley shuts up. He says, his long fingers stroking the top of his cane, "Who am I? Oh no, dear Ashley. I think the question most certainly is 'who are YOU?'" The thing chuckles and cocks his head. "To your second point, I shall indeed let you out of here, if you can make it to the end. And while *I* won't stop you or interfere . . . well, you'll find the inhabitants here a bit . . . more engaged than I am." He giggles and his laugh seems to circle in front of him and run around the room, too.

Paul says, "Is there something in here that wants to . . . kill us?"

Besides this freaky ass-wad in front of us, Paul?

The thing stops again and then flicks his head to the pocket door. Suddenly, we hear the squeak of metal on metal again and something pounds on the door—one solid, heavy pound. We back away from the door together, but that brings us closer to the thing so I whirl around and the thing flicks his hand up in a "stop" motion. The pounding and metal stop.

"Very few things do not," says the thing. The demon. Or whatever it is. Then his lips curl. "I will say, though, some are less inclined toward destruction and still fight the good fight. However pointless. They are cursed by that which turns all poor souls into raving lunatics: hope."

He looks at his fingernails again, which are really just talons. "Anyway, of course, a perfect Five is my hope for my collection. But I will say this. It may be that not all of you can make it out. It may be that only some of you can win. If I were you . . ." and then he stops to do a little giggle again, "well, I'd make sure I was one who did." He looks up at us again and his red eyes swirl. "Survival of the fittest and all that."

I say, my voice shaking, too, "What if we win? What happens then?"

The thing raises his eyebrows like he hasn't even considered it. "Oh. I guess you get . . . your pathetic little lives and lies back." He shrugs. "I haven't really thought about it, to be perfectly honest, dearest Gretchen." He looks at me almost kindly. "That's just a darling question, though." He continues moving around the room, "But now I'm afraid anything else I tell you will ruin the surprise and we can't have that, can we? So, my dears, I leave you to discover the infinite treasures here by yourselves."

Then he giggles again and stops by the scene of The Sleeper, which is winding down like a toy running low on batteries.

He says, "Good luck, dearest Five. I look forward to seeing you soon." He giggles then wiggles his fingers at us. "Bye-bye."

And with a pop, he—the man, the thing, the monster—is gone.

I let out a breath I didn't know I was holding in.

The scene in The Sleeper has stopped. The skeleton and demon are permanently out of their hiding spots.

No one speaks for a full minute. Violet whimpers and Paul bends down, putting his hands on his knees like he's catching his breath.

Dylan says, "Holy bejesus, please let us out of here what the fuck was that thing what the fuck," in one continuous monotone.

Ashley says, "What just happened? Who was that? WHAT was that?"

Paul swallows and stands up. "Whatever that thing was, it's pretty clear we have to keep going. We need to get out. And I don't think we can go back." As if in answer, another loud thump knocks against the door.

I say, my voice smaller than usual, "That thing wasn't human."

Ashley says, "Duh." But her voice is small, too.

Violet, her voice quiet but fast and intense, says, "Um, maybe we could try the door to the Wheel House part again. Maybe this is all a joke or something. Maybe we just need to go get a House employee and have them open the door. We should try our cell phones again—"

She doesn't get a chance to finish her sentence. The sharp crack of an axe chopping through wood interrupts her.

DYLAN

The Sleeper has started its clicking thingy again, but this time the little douchetroll laughs, shrill, like a freak maniac. Another axe hit splinters the wood.

I grab Gretch's monster bag and we fly through to the next room of the House. We are bringing up the rear and no thank you, I do not want to be the caboose of this hell train so I pull Gretch along, but she is dragging. She is looking for the door of this next room. I let go of her bag and let her do it. She finds another pocket door and slams it shut just as we hear a mad crash of wood and the creep of metal.

Jesus, oh help me, Jesus.

Who knew all it took was a demon House to finally make me pray for real?

The group stops as a shitload of glass crashes at both ends of this new room we're in. I hear a horse's whinny. And then jangly calliope music fills the entire room, like a GD joke.

But below all that, I hear a growl.

We are in the Streets of Yore, a part of the House I loved as a kid. Gretch would love it, too, if it weren't for the fact that there are dolls running around now—dozens and dozens more than in the Wheel House. Plus there's a dog. It stands in front of us with its fur raised up, foam bearding its mouth. Rabid? Yes. I would have to say yes.

Paul puts his arms out like a crossing guard. Quietly he says, "Don't move."

The dog steps closer. Growling, hackles hackling. Fuck-a-doodle-doo. Death by Dalmatian was not how I pictured my end. Not cool, doggy, not cool. When you walk into the Streets of Yore section, you know, on the days when the things in it aren't alive, there are fake storefronts with old-timey shops and places. One of the first places you see is a fire station where this dog must have come from. And behind that, of course, shops full of dolls. I can hear little feet pitter-pattering.

But the dog. The dog is angry and panting and not pattering or laughing. Or small. Or sane. There's a break in the music and behind the door in back of us I can hear the squeak of metal and know that the knight is walking across the other room. Squeak, stomp. Squeak, stomp. Growl. Hackles. A knight with an axe or a rabid dog?

Choices can be a bitch.

The dog crouches down like he's going to lunge and Paul spreads his arms out wider like that will stop a rabid dog from eating us, and then all five of us grab onto each other and I squeeze my eyes shut, just waiting for the doggy chomp.

Instead, a loud doggy yelp happens.

When I open my eyes, the dog has dolls all over him. He gets one in his mouth and shakes it, then starts running down the hallway past the storefronts. Gretch and I look at each other. Her gorgeous eyes are wide, and her pupils are way dilated. At least we won't be eaten? By a dog anyway.

Ashley says, "We need to put something in front of the door."

I look around for something and then Paul points to the storefronts to the right of us and a little behind the ramp we're standing on. The rooms used to have dolls and now just have blown out windows. My eyes land on a dresser.

"The dresser," I say and I jump over the white railing of the ramp. Paul jumps, too, and we crunch-step on broken glass and enter the room.

Another thump.

Violet says, "Um, can you hurry, guys?" Which for Violet is, like, *Move mothereffers!* So we move.

We each take an end of a dresser and drag it up the ramp, Gretchen, Violet, and Ashley joining in on the pushing. After what seems like hours, we make it to the door to the other room and push it in front of the pocket door.

My lungs hurt. Note: no more weed for me. *Jesus,* I think, *I swear I'll be good. Mostly.*

But then we hear an axe chop. We hear it get stuck in the dresser and I cringe all over. I can see the dresser moving a little like the knight on the other end is trying to wiggle out the axe. But then the dresser sits still.

Thank you, Jesus. I'll work on that good thing, yo.

I take a deep breath and turn around to the room in front of us. The music starts up again and all of us jump. Freaky ass circus music attacks our ears. We're still on the ramp. Every once in a while, the sound of feet pattering above us and around us pokes through the music, but there aren't any dolls anywhere I can see. The floor is cobblestone and there are trees on either side of the street. And I swear I can see a crow clocking us with its beady little crow eyes from one of the branches. Storefront after storefront and houses line each side of the fake street. When I look up at the fake houses and the fake windows, I see doll faces looking out, then ducking back inside. No mad doggy at least. So. There's that.

I catch eyes with Paul and he shakes his head. Even Ashley has nothing to say. Every one of us is pale as shit.

Gretch's mouth is a straight line. Finally, she says, "Well. I guess we have to go forward." The freaky music stops again.

She looks around, "Ashley, you've been here before, right? Or Violet?"

Violet nods and so does Ashley, though she is looking up at the windows and watching a doll stare at her, its face stuck in a creeptastic smile.

"Jesus," she murmurs. I don't think the girl is praying.

Violet says, "Yeah. This is just a street of old-timey things. You know?"

Paul says, "Does everything come alive here?"

I shrug. "Dude didn't say, but it sure looks like it." Then I swallow and ask a question that has been bothering me. "Was that, like, the devil?" I think of all the times I didn't pay attention in Sunday school or the times I made fun of church shit.

Dear Jesus, I think. *So sorry, dude. Are we cool?*

Gretch furrows her brow. "I thought you don't believe in the devil."

I shrug again and say, "I mean, that dude was pretty evil-looking, right?"

Paul mutters something like, "Hell is empty and all the devils are here." I can't disagree.

Violet pipes up, "But he said everything in here has choices, right? I mean, maybe something is going to help us?"

Gretch exhales. "Violet, give it up. We're screwed."

Paul nods and gives puppy dog eyes to Violet; universal dude for *Sorry*. "I think Gretchen might be right," he says. "I don't know what's going on, but I don't trust anything that whatever-it-was guy said."

Ashley starts down the ramp, her heels clicking, then turns around. "Listen, you guys can jerk off about the theology of all this, but I want out. And we aren't even close to being done with this place. Plus, we don't know where that dog went. Or when that knight will fucking break through the door . . ." Girl's eyes are bright and shiny like quarters. Or eyes with tears in them. "We don't know when and why things start attacking . . . This whole fucking House is alive, do you understand?" She turns on her heel and takes a step and a doll runs past her, almost knocking her over. She pauses, tilts her head, huffs out, but then keeps going.

We look at each other. And then follow.

What else are we going to do?

ASHLEY

Fuck this place. It can go straight to hell. I don't deserve something like this. My dad's going to be a senator. A SENATOR. The rest of these losers . . . whatever. But my family made this state. Someone is going to pay. Someone is going to PAY, goddamn it!

I walk down the ramp with some purpose, finally—to Get The Fuck Out Of Here—but then step on the cobblestone and my heel gets caught between stones.

For some reason, this is what makes me lose it.

I stop and scream, my arms by my sides. I take off my shoe and fling it down the hall. Then I take the other one off and fling it, too. The music has stopped and in the silence, the shoes hit farther down the hall and echo loud. There's a pause, then a hundred little voices start laughing. I look up at one of the fake house windows. Three dolls look down at me from a railing, their stupid doll faces and flat eyes just . . . staring. Where the laugh comes from, beats the fuck out of me. Which somehow makes their awful faces and the disembodied laugh that much worse.

I feel a hand on my arm. It's Violet. Her hand is soft.

She says, in that quiet voice of hers, "Let's just keep moving."

I sniffle and wipe my eyes, then smooth out my skirt and nod. Everyone gathers around me.

Dylan says, "I think we need to stick together."

I disagree. I think *I* need to get out of here this goddamn minute no matter what. But I don't say that out loud.

We walk a couple of feet and between two storefronts there's a glass case with three puppet-like figures. There's a sign: THE MAGICIAN'S CORNER.

It whirs into motion.

The one in the middle is a wizard-y thing and stands behind a table, a hat in one hand. With jerky mechanical movements, he lifts up the hat to reveal a rabbit, then down, then up to reveal a ball, then down, up to reveal dice and down, and on and on. The two other guys have instruments and they play them, but no sound comes out. The hat comes up and reveals a severed head, eyes bloody. The wizard looks at us and laughs and the hat comes down.

"This place isn't very nice," Violet says as we move away fast, like a herd of dumbasses. Her voice echoes down the hall. Somehow the silence is worse than the crazy music.

I snort and say, "Duh," but my heart isn't in it and I just swallow and move on with everyone else.

We pass a barbershop on one side, the red and blue pole thingy twirling as we pass by. On the other side is a sheriff's office, a hand stuck in liquid in a jar on a writing desk, the fingers wiggling. Gross. Next is a woodcarving place, inside are puppets in various stages of finish. When we pass by, the parts click together and bop up and down. The puppets are missing hands and feet, parts of faces. I shiver. My bare feet slap against the cold cobblestone. But damn they feel better.

"Goodness, it seems you are lost at sea, doesn't it?"

The voice is creaky and old-fashioned, like a school-marm and an opera-singer combined. I look up. There's a wooden woman sticking out of the top of the woodcarving storefront. And she's looking down at us with an expression that looks almost nice.

Violet looks up, eyes all hopeful. "Can you help us, ma'am?"

Idiot. I snap at her—I can't help it. "You're talking to wood, you idiot. Try not to be pathetic."

Violet shrinks back but the woman tsks at me. "You should really mind your manners, you know."

A hysterical laugh bursts out of me. "Manners? Everything here is trying to kill us!" I can't help the octave of my voice. It goes higher than I could have imagined.

The wooden woman smiles and says cheerily, "Yes. Though not all of us have such ignoble intentions, this ship is full to the gunwales of angry spirits, my dears."

Great. Maybe we'll be sea-metaphored to death . . .

Before I say anything back, a doll jumps down from the tree and lands on her neck. The wooden woman tries to smile. "A crew united can be stronger than the tide, you know. All you must do is—"

The doll wraps itself around her face, cutting the nice woman's words off.

Crew united, my ass.

But still I move closer to everyone. I can smell Gretchen's lavender scent right near me. And then the calliope music starts again. It's coming from a huge area at the end of the hall filled with brass instruments and drums. A band that is playing by itself.

Of course it is.

We move away from the lady toward the music. Because where else are we supposed to go?

Though we see dolls' faces peering at us in the storefronts and through branches—and I swear at least one crow—they don't attack. We pass a statuary, an apothecary with medieval looking medical equipment, a lamp place, glassware . . . a cart with peanuts and popcorn.

Dylan runs up to it. "Suh-weet! Starved, yo," he says over the music. He grabs a handful of popcorn and shoves it in his mouth.

No, no, no, I think. Dumbass.

"How could you be hungry at a time like this?" Gretchen snaps, suddenly all mom-like. "And how do you know it's not poisoned, Dylan?" She strides over to him and knocks the popcorn out of his hand.

His cheeks are full, like a chipmunk's.

"Spit it out." Gretchen points at the floor.

Instead, Dylan swallows and smiles. "Last time I was here it wasn't even real."

And then the room feels like it gets 60 degrees cooler. Because Gretchen's face is so dark I'm positive a storm has just rolled in. Lightning is about to strike. The girl is hot when she's mad. But man, I'm so glad it's not me she's mad at. I mean, I could handle her, sure, but Dylan? How he has survived this long is beyond me.

"You said you've never been here," Gretchen hisses, her voice low and dangerous. She glances around. Our eyes meet for a second and I look away. I guess the lovers aren't as solid as they look. A delicious jolt passes through me, but I tamp it down. Not possible. Still, lightning has struck twice today . . . and we are in some demon House with, you know, SENTIENT DOLLS. So, stranger things have clearly happened. Are happening.

Dylan is stalling, but before he can say anything, there's a whinny and a huge cracking sound and wood explodes out from a storefront down the hall. A horse comes out of nowhere and runs by us, neighing. We turn as it passes us, the wind blowing my hair back. But the horse has nowhere to go so it runs by us again and disappears around the corner. Six or seven dolls come out of nowhere and run after it.

A horse.

The calliope music stops again and a whirring mechanical sound like The Sleeper reaches us.

Down by the exploded stable is a fortuneteller chick in a glass box with some symbol on the side. I can see from here that she has blonde hair. She turns her face to us and she is super pretty and kind-looking.

"Come get your fortune. Madame Josefina will tell you your fate."

Her voice is sweet and melodic, especially in the silence of the place. No calliope music. No tiny footsteps. For a minute, I have a little bit of hope.

Violet says in a whisper, "I hope it's good."

For once, I don't snap at her.

VIOLET

I have had some seriously surreal moments in my life:

In the 4th grade, after I'd won the regional spelling bee for my age group, an adult judge took me aside when no one was looking and said, "You think you're pretty f—ing smart, don't you?" The joke was on her, though. I never think I'm smart.

In 8th grade I walked in on my parents having sex.

That one thing I will never tell anyone about ever that is still happening.

Paul flirted with me.

But I can honestly say, this House wins by a gazillion trillion. Cosine to the power of googolplex. Or something. I got an A- in calculus until I brought it up to an A. Anyway, what I'm trying to say is:

Oh. My. God.

I mean, maybe number 2 comes close to this moment, but never has any animatronic thing talked to me and never have I hoped more than anything that the animated inanimate object in front of me would tell me whether or not I would survive a House of horrors.

At least I'll die with a beautiful boy?

We've all walked to the pretty blonde woman in the fortune-teller box as she starts turning over tarot cards. Her eyes are huge and, purple, and slightly upturned. She makes little noises, "mm-hmm," "ah!" and "oh no." Her brows furrow and every once in a while she looks up and gives us a nice smile.

I move closer to the box to see the cards. When I started doing that one thing I will never talk about to anyone ever, I actually took an online course on the tarot. I kept asking the cards if I should be doing what I was doing. They always said no, because, you know, I shouldn't be. Anyway, I'm no expert, but I know the cards pretty well so I lean in to get a closer look.

The first card is the Devil.

Then the Tower.

Then Death.

Madame Josefina sighs and says, eyes kind and sorrowful, "Your fortune is coming." The box makes a whirring sound and then a cha-ching and a card shoots out at the bottom.

Gretchen picks it up and reads it, her eyebrows furrowing. She looks at Madame Josefina. Then she drops the card. It lands face up.

You are all going to die in here, it reads.

The fortuneteller laughs. She cackles, actually. She cackles loud and her face turns mean and ugly in an instant. "You're all going to die in here. You're all going to die!" She yells and smacks a be-ringed hand against the glass box. The entire thing starts clunking back and forth like someone is trying to move it from the inside and then the calliope music starts up again. I yelp and step back and right at that moment, the horse comes running back in, covered in dolls. Dolls are pulling its ears, clinging to all four legs. It's like a horse made of dolls now. It rears up and shakes its front legs, its eyes wide and terrified. The dolls shoot off like fireworks.

Dylan appears out of nowhere with a branch and gets close enough to the horse to start batting off dolls. "Don't . . . be . . . mean . . . to . . . horses," he's yelling as he bats them off and they go flying. Gretchen runs to the nearest tree and works to tear off a branch. After a second, Paul runs to a tree, too. Ashley has somehow found a shoe for smacking dolls. But a heel gets caught in one of the dolls' hair, so Ashley swings it around and sends it flying, the shoe stuck in the doll's head.

I need a branch. But before I go to grab one, I turn to Madame Josefina who is just laughing now, eyes wide and crazy. I point my finger at her, "You are a terrible fortuneteller. That's not what that reading said at all. You are terrible at this!" For a minute, she gets a look of genuine hurt on her face and she says, "Nuh-uh" but I can't answer because something jumps on my shoulders and I scream. The calliope music stops again and I can hear Gretchen, Paul, and Dylan screaming, too. And I hear a crash of wood and the far off squeak of armor.

The knight has made it through.

The thing on my shoulders won't let go. And then a searing lightning pain shoots through my ear. I realize this thing is going to rip my ear off. There's warm liquid running down my neck—I know that it is blood—and my ear is on fire. I am all panic as I try to reach around and grab it, when I feel a whack that knocks me forward on to my knees. It knocks the thing off, too.

The searing pain vanishes and in its place is a burning. I'm still on my knees and something flashes in the corner of my eye so I sink into myself and look up in time to see the underbelly of the horse and its legs flying over me. I feel the whoosh as the horse jumps over me—now free of dolls but clearly still panicked. It races straight to the end of the hall and runs right over the knight and through the door the knight just splintered.

I put a hand up to my ear and feel warm sticky blood and torn skin . . . and then Paul is helping me up.

The dolls have formed a line—more like a mob—near the storefronts. Gretchen and Dylan stand with branches raised like baseball bats, panting hard, facing them. Ashley stands near them with crazy eyes and a doll head dangling by its hair in one hand.

The dolls, way eerie in the sudden silence, look terrifying, because always and forever dolls are TERRIFYING anyway even when they're not animated by some dark, demonic force. But in this really messed up House, they are WAY WORSE. Their faces are still doll-like and unchanging and their eyes are totally void of anything but they are still somehow STARING at us and it's clear they want us dead.

They start moving toward us . . .

Paul and I look at each other and say at the same time, "RUN!"

PAUL

Once again, we are sprinting through a room away from dolls—DOLLS—under a sign that says SEA STORY and straight toward a ramp with a picture of a blue whale and an arrow pointing up the ramp.

I can't even imagine what is in here. Hopefully there are no sea dolls in here or something.

Dolls, man.

All five of us make it through the room and then Ashley finds the pocket door and slams it shut. We can hear the dolls throwing themselves at the door. Thwunk thwunk thwunk, I'm thinking Shakespeare: *When sorrows come, they come not single spies, But in battalions.* I am hardcore wishing for my fake sword right about now. Anything pointy.

The ramp twists around and there are pictures of all types of whales on the walls. Orca whale. Sperm whale. Killer whale.

A sound of *whoosh whoosh* comes through when the thwunking dolls aren't taking up all our ear real estate. We stop halfway up the ramp.

Gretchen turns to Dylan and says hard, "What's in *this* room, *Dylan?*"

Dylan ignores the question and moves toward Violet, eyes concerned. "Dudette is bleeding."

I remember Violet with that doll attached to her ear and my adrenaline kicks in again. The anger, the fear—all of it is familiar. I have never been so scared in my life, except for that one time with my dad.

I turn to her. "How is your ear?" I ask.

I wonder if I should hold her hand again?

"I hope they aren't attracted to blood," Ashley mutters.

Gretchen whirls around. Her eyes are blazing. "Jesus, Ashley! Could you be any more selfish, you self-centered piece of—"

Violet bursts into tears, silencing all of us.

I take her in my arms. I can't help myself; it's instinct. Gentle Violet. I can feel her whole body trembling and it makes me want to cry, too. But she doesn't pull away.

Shakespeare love quotes swim around in my head:

The very first instant that I saw you did my heart fly to your service. And:

Love looks not with the eyes, but with the mind, and therefore is winged Cupid painted blind.

Pure beauty, these words, like Violet herself. But what comes out of my mouth?

"Hey. You're okay. It's okay. Gotta buck up, okay?"

She leans back away from my arms with a little frown.

Smooth.

Violet wipes her eyes, smearing a bit of blood on her cheekbone. Is it weird that she looks even cuter? Gretchen comes up to her and pats her arm awkwardly. Ashley is instantly on the other side, clearing her throat.

"I hope you're okay, or whatever," Ashley says.

We all stare at her. Ashley looks down at her fingernails, all of a sudden engrossed in a paint chip.

Violet does one final wipe of her nose. "I'm fine."

Then Dylan appears. He's holding something out to Violet and it takes me a second to see that he's ripped a swath of his T-shirt all along the bottom. His clothes are always stupid long, so his shirt looks like it's a normal length now.

"Hey, yo, we can wrap this around your head to stop the bleeding," he says.

She smiles through her tears. He smiles back.

"You'll look like a badass warrior," he adds.

Why didn't I think of ripping off part of me for her? Stupid Paul. Stupid stupid.

Violet laughs a hiccup laugh. "That's me," she says. "A warrior."

We all start laughing. Violet the warrior. How funny. But then Dylan wraps the shirt around her head and with the blood and the wrap, and damn if she doesn't look like some beautiful warrior goddess.

"You guys were awesome with those dolls," she says to Dylan. "That was smart to grab a branch."

He shrugs. I am totally aware of how close they are standing and how he just ministered to her like some romantic hero in a play. I feel a lightning surge of jealousy—sharp enough that it hurts. I step closer before I can stop myself.

"I knocked that doll off your head," I say like an idiot.

I, caveman. You, woman.

What is wrong with me?

Dylan, because he seems to know the score, steps back from Violet, his foot making a squelching sound. He gives me a look. *I'm not moving in*, is what it says. *Just being nice.* Despite myself, I like this guy. He's actually really cool and, like, kind. And now I wish I would have stopped people from slamming him into lockers back at school. Or even had the courage to just say something. But. Survival. What I always say to myself to make myself feel better. But a squirmy feeling makes me roll my shoulders around and shift on my feet. Which are suddenly freezing and cold and wet. Now I'm faced with real survival, the fake one seems, well . . . fake.

"Hey. There's water here." Dylan says, looking down.

We all do the same. Sure enough, we are standing in about a half inch of water. The *whoosh whoosh* sound seems to be getting louder.

"Oh god," Ashley says. Her face is bright white.

Gretchen snorts. "What? Your hair will frizz out?"

Ashley swallows and doesn't even say anything bitchy. She just groans. "This room. This next room."

Violet's eyes go wide. "Oh no," she says.

Dylan says, "The whale."

Ashley says, "The squid."

Gretchen seems to get it as soon as I do. She slumps against the wall. "Please tell me they're figurines?"

No one speaks.

GRETCHEN

"You'll love this place." That's what he said to me. Never mind the fact that the little shit lied about having been here before. Dylan. You are truly going to get your ass kicked. Truly. Why oh why did you lie? I don't ask for much. Just loyalty and, you know, not being lied to.

Violet, with her head wrap on, and who actually does look kind of like a righteous killer ninja in it, says, "They're . . . big."

"Of course they're big," I say and slump more. I put my head against the wall and rub my eyes.

Ashley sniffles. There are tears in her eyes. Real tears. I'd almost feel sorry for her—pretty faces and tears can do that to me. But not quite. She's too much of a bitch-hole for any compassion to stick.

"They're more than big," Ashley says. "I don't know how we're going to get out of this room."

Paul says, "Whatever they are, they may not be . . . alive . . . or whatever."

Violet nods, her face brightening. "Yeah! We don't know when things start moving. Maybe we can run through this section and get to the end. We do not want to . . . go up against this room." She puts her hand on her ear. The blood is soaking through the bandage. It must hurt like a mofo.

Better than fighting, though? Running like hell. "Yes. Let's try to sprint through this room. Is it pretty straightforward? Like a straight shot?"

Ashley shakes her head. "No, it's a ramp like this one. We follow this ramp and then there's the entrance to the room. And then another ramp around the edges of the whole room leads us up and out of this section. But we have to go up that big ramp in the room—it's the only way out. Right past the . . ." She stops talking and shakes her head again.

I sigh. "Of course. Well. We're just going to have to run fast." But after I say it, I start worrying about Dylan. He's not exactly a model of health, that one. He went through a cigarette smoking phase when he was younger and he's still in his weed phase, so his lungs aren't awesome. Plus, he weighs about 4 pounds, and most of that is bone. I look at him. I can see he is thinking the same thing. His eyes shine at mine through his eyeliner.

I give him this look, *You can do this, dude.*

He answers back with his own look, *I'm going to have to, dudette.*

If only I didn't love him so, the little shit liar.

I stand up straight. "Okay. Let's do it." I start wading up the ramp. Only now do I realize the water is now about ankle height. Fuckity fuck fuck. Water seeps through my shoes. Great find at Lulu's Vintage in the Twin Cities when I visited last year, looking at fashion schools. Asshole House. It owes me another pair of these shoes.

Then I get to the entrance of the room. I can see why Ashley lost it.

In front of us is an ocean. Or, what is supposed to be a fake ocean, I imagine. Only it's not a fake ocean and it's starting to lap out of the little enclosure it's built into.

But that's not the worst part. Feet and feet and feet above us, a ginormous whale and what looks like a huge fucking squid are locked in some embrace.

"Oh shit," I whisper, and stop.

The ramp is built around the outside of the room and it circles up and up and around and around the whale and the squid. Just like Ashley said. The only way out is up the ramp.

The water in the place is splashing around, real and wet and deep. There's a guy in a boat on the water, but he isn't moving so I guess he's fake like the whale and squid. I heave a sigh of relief. *Stay that way you sea sons of bitches. Stay that way.*

I jump when a music machine at the far end of the room starts playing "Under the Sea."

Now it's just the shushing sound of the water in front of us and the manic music from the machine. And something else.

Squeaks. Almost like screams.

I flip around, my eyes wide. Is it those dolls again? I see Violet wince and cover her ear.

But then something flies in front of me and when I turn back around I see it's a seagull. There are seagulls swooping around. And a crow.

Ashley says in my ear, her teeth clenched, breath hot, "Let's go. Now."

For once, we are in agreement. I nod and look back at Dylan, who is rocking from foot to foot, eyes darting around, chewing on a finger. My anxiety climbs.

Come on, Dylan, baby, you can do it. I still have to kill you for lying to me and then figure out why you did. I turn back around.

"Now!" I say and start the sprint up the ramp.

To the right of me is the giant cavern of water and whale, and to the left are glass cases full of huge model ships and other random sea shit. But all I pay attention to is the seagulls and the eye of the squid getting nearer.

Right when I reach the eye, it blinks.

Dylan says, "Oh shit."

And then the room explodes.

DYLAN

I am suddenly aware—like a G-Damn prophet of God—that I am not going to get out of this room alive.

And peace descends upon me like an angel on high.

Only it's not peace and it's no angel. It's a motherfucking squid leg that slams down in front of me, splintering the wood of the ramp. I throw up my arms to protect my face and a huge wood chunk sticks into my forearm. I rip it out and scream. Water starts to pool deep in the ramp gash. Blood pools in my arm gash.

Ow, fuckity, ouch, Squid!

Ashley, Paul, Violet, and my Gretch are running ahead. I am stuck behind a slimy squid leg and my arm feels like it's going to fall off.

If I yell, though, Gretch will try to come back for me. No way I'm putting her in danger.

One thing my baby is not is a scared-y cat. She'd kill herself saving someone she loves, especially her family. *I'm* her family.

And then I know, right there, right with a stinking squid leg blocking my run and my arm about to fall off that the girl I'm in love with totally *does* love me like family.

Like a brother.

Luckily, before I have to look that monster in the face, the real monster in front of me lifts up its leg and a huge pool of water is now between me and the dry ramp the rest of my crew is still sprinting up.

I look at the water.

So . . . I never technically learned to swim. Like, not really. I mean, my parents took me and shit because they're good parents and wanted me to do everything, but I never actually *went*. I mean, I was 10 and just getting into skater shit. And smoking.

But I realize now is not the time to think about missed moments and shit. Time to swim, motherfucker, because ain't no other way around this calamari. Before I can think too hard, I crouch down, take a deep breath, and jump—making sure to hit up my man before I hit the water.

Jesus? Please . . . just please don't let Gretch notice me. Let her get out of here.

And then my head is underwater and I open my eyes. I can see squid squidding around and a whale belly bellying. They're stuck on the floor basically, because there's not enough water. Except we are all getting moved up so I'm guessing there's more water happening somehow . . .

And then I am frightfully fucking aware that I can't breathe.

I paddle-paddle-paddle and my lungs are screaming so hard and pain shoots through my arm. And then finally, finally, my head is out of the water and I gulp in a big breath. But the screaming is still happening and I realize it's Gretch, who has now noticed I'm gone.

Jesusssss, Dude, You are not holding up your end of our bargain.

She is at the top of the splintered ramp, which has spread out further because of the rising water level, and one arm is being held by Paul who is sitting on the ramp with his feet dug in and pulling at Gretch while she reaches her other hand toward me. Ashley is halfway up the ramp still going and Violet is standing there with her badass warrior wrap and her hands over her mouth. But Gretch, Gretch . . . She's going to fall in the water coming after me. Not cool. Most def not cool.

"Gretch, go!" I try to yell. I swallow a huge gulp of ocean water and go down again. This time, I can't move; my arm is like numb deadweight now, and I'm mad panicked that Gretch is going to fall in. But then, the squid leg plunges into the water directly in front of me. The thing wraps me up and launches me in the air.

I am sailing. I am flying. I am BREATHING, so that's pretty cool, even if I am being hugged by a giant squid. The world is small below and I see everyone from above—Gretch by the ramp, Paul holding on, Violet looking up at me, mouth in an "O," Ashley now fighting with something in some weird space suit or something way far up—and I think for one silly, giddy, squiddy second, "Thanks, Squid!!"

But then I land in the water again. This time by the whale.

Well, shit.

The squid lets go of me, but now the whale is rolling and I am close to going under that gigantic belly. On the other side of me is a giant eye.

Whale body or squid eye? Choices. I do not like the choices in this House.

I close my eyes and try to will my body to stop fighting and clawing for breath and to just, like, GIVE IN, because this shit is pointless to try to fight against because, you know, squid eye or whale belly, but then something grabs my shirt and hauls me out of the water and into a boat. The boat we saw when we first entered the room. With the fisherman dude. Who is now fully alive.

And so am I. I breathe in so huge my rib cage hurts.

I look at the grizzled-looking man in a floppy hat and a yellow rain slicker and dude yells something at me, but I can't hear him because the noise of everything else drowns him out. The whale bellows a loud-as-fuck primal scream and I see we are right by his teeth. His really, really big teeth. Fisher dude picks up a paddle and starts paddling backwards.

I can still hear Gretch yelling, "Dylan!" but now from way up above me. Water splashes into the boat—we are riding some big waves and we hit against the wall halfway up because the water level has gotten higher. The giant motherfucking animals aren't higher though, on account of how big they are, so at least there's that. I guess.

The guy yells at me again. This time I'm able to get what he's asking me.

"Where's your boat, son?"

I shake my head and wipe water out of my eyes. "I need to get to my friends!" I scream, pointing straight up, behind the whale head. The whale's tail slaps down and splinters the ramp on the side where Gretch was.

I scream, "NO!!!!" But I look up and I can see seagulls and Gretch's face over the railing way, way up the ramp so I know she's safe.

"There," I point and try to get up. "I need to get there!"

The fisherman shakes his head at me like I'm crazy. "Son, that just ain't going to happen. And anyway, up there ain't much better."

He points and now the whale head isn't in the way and I see that Ashley is still fighting with the guy in the space suit. Only she's been joined by everyone else, too. Gretch is half fighting then half leaning over the railing to look at me.

And then right by her, the guy in the space suit somehow shakes off Violet and Paul and walks with Ashley held over his head like he's going to throw her into the whale mouth.

Dude's right: Up there ain't much better.

ASHLEY

I am not going to die like this. I am NOT GOING TO DIE LIKE THIS! How embarrassing would this be?

But the gross looking guy in an old-fashioned scuba suit—the kind you see on the covers of beat-up library paperbacks from, like, the 1940s or whatever—is holding me straight up like I'm a barbell. And he's LAUGHING. He's going to throw me into the whale's mouth. I can see huge teeth, a pink squirming tongue. I'm going to be chunky krill for this fucking whale. I am pretty sure I'm peeing myself.

For a minute, time stops and I can feel everything. I stop screaming.

There is an honest to god *ocean wind* in here. It rustles my hair and I can smell fish and seagulls and saltwater and deep, decaying things I do not want to smell. Seagulls are swarming around us and I hear their screeches and a caw. For some reason, I notice my purse by this thing's feet along with the glass that burst out from the case he was trapped in and I say, "Hey. There's my Gucci purse."

And then I am whipped backward. Hard.

Time starts up again, this time on fast-forward. I land on a model boat in one of the blown-out cases. Wood slices into my back. My head bounces off the wall. In front of me, Paul is wrestling with the thing in the suit on the ramp floor and Violet is biting its hand. Out of nowhere, Gretchen appears and punt-kicks the thing's head. It stops laughing and its eyes close. I notice, for whatever reason, she's lost her monster bag. Gretchen stands there—girl is pale—hair sticking straight up, looking more than a little wild. Her chest is heaving and her eyes are on fire. Despite everything, my heart races, and for once in this House it's not from fear.

I stand up fast. Too fast. I almost go back down again. My head throbs and I feel a huge bump on the back of my skull. I pick a splinter of wood out of my arm. In front of me, glass litters the ramp. But there's no time to be picky because we're losing ramp real estate to a flood. And that scuba-diver-thing has opened its eyes again.

"Let's go!" I scream and step right on glass as I get out of the case. I gasp as sharp, stabbing pain shoots through both feet. I take a step on one foot and almost pass out. Another step. Must move toward exit. Ow, ow, ow. Fuck. Ow.

Gretchen turns to me. "We can't leave Dylan!" she yells.

I hesitate.

The whale is splashing around and I can't see Dylan anywhere. The ramp shifts under my feet in the sort of scary way that says shit's going down.

"Screw this," I say out loud to no one, and hobble as fast as I can up the ramp on the sides of my feet, the pain ebbing while my panic's flowing.

I am not dying for some tweaker ass. Or even for whatever the fuck Gretchen is to me. Or for any of these losers. *They're losers!* I tell myself. Losers.

That demon guy's words echo in my ear as I limp up the ramp, not looking back on purpose.

Survival of the fittest.

I'M the fittest. I am getting out. I AM GETTING OUT OF HERE.

But something else wrestles with my head space. They did save me from whatever that scuba guy was. They could have run. They could have let him/it kill me. A tiny voice adds: *Maybe you would have even deserved it.* I tell that tiny voice to "fuck off"—out loud. In spite of the pain, I climb the ramp faster. I'm almost to the top. This isn't socialism. The demon guy laid it out: Eat or be eaten. There's no such thing as an even playing field and if you need help you're clearly weak and maybe you should die and sucks to be you, stupid assholes, why should *I* help—

And then I hear Gretchen again: "Dylan, hold on!"

Despite myself, I stop and turn around.

That scuba-guy thing is being pinned down by what used to be statues of sea captains. They'd been standing on top of the glass cases but since those broke, they must have fallen off. They are small and dignified looking, and holy balls, they are huffing and puffing as they work to keep him/it down.

Hope shoots through me. Are they . . . helping us? Then the scuba guy starts laughing again. Even over the roar of the sea, the laugh gives me chills.

But of greater importance is Dylan dangling from a rope held by Paul, Gretchen, and Violet. I can see he's slipping. He's going to fall right into the mouth of the whale. And if not that, then straight into the water where he'll most likely be crushed.

If one of them lets go of the rope to grab him, I'm guessing the whole effort would fall apart. Dylan can't be that heavy, but the thrashing and the wind and the wobbly ramp won't let them move.

I sigh.

Fucking moochers. Gretchen better thank me for this.

I run back as fast as I can on the sides of my feet and reach the group just as Dylan reaches up a hand to grab the slick railing. He hits it but his hand slips off and he's going to fall.

I leap toward him and jackknife my body on the railing. My breath whooshes out of me and the world spins upside down. I'm staring into the mouth of a giant whale.

But I get his hand and hold on tight.

His hand is wet and is *slllliiippping* down and I almost lose him but he shoots his other arm toward me and I get a look at his face for an instant. His eyes are bright and wide and scared as fuck and there is eyeliner trailing down his face.

His other hand grabs on to me and we now have a four-hand locked grip, so I've got him. But then, oh shit, I feel my body flipping over the railing.

You better eat me fast, Whaley. I squeeze my eyes shut.

Someone grabs my belt; someone else grabs my feet; Gretchen grabs onto my arms, and Dylan and I are pulled back slowly over the railing. All five of us collapse in a heap. A sweaty, panting, not-so-wonderful smelling heap. Alive, though.

We stand up, and at that exact moment, the whale's tail slams down again and knocks the ramp out right below us. I fall on my butt, hard, and someone half lands on me. But my eyes are on Gretchen who is half in the water and hanging on to the ramp.

Out of nowhere, Dylan sprints to her and pulls her out fast like a goddamn suburban mom lifting a car off her baby. The whole room is splinters and whale and squid and the scuba guy and the sea captains seem to be somewhere in the water. The whale has started thrashing in earnest now and squid tentacles smash into the walls above us and rumble below us. Glass breaks from what seems like a million different cases. We have maybe 15 feet of ramp to run up to get to the next door. Violet is in the lead up above. She's lost the bloody rag on her head, the one that made her look like the hero of a revolution. But her eyes are full panic and she yells for the millionth time, "Run!"

So I do.

VIOLET

We make it up the ramp. Somehow, some way, we make it up.
Once Ashley limps through—her feet are so bloody—I slam the
door shut and lock it.

My lungs hurt. My ear hurts. My face hurts. I have scrapes
everywhere, a large rash down one of my sides from who knows
what. Saltwater stings my eyes, makes my ear scream.

I don't even want to look in this room. I don't even want to
know what's in here.

I put my head on my knees and wrap my arms around my
legs.

I can't deal with this. We're not even close to being through
this House. Whatever is in here can just kill me now.

A big, gasping sob shakes through me.

I feel wet arms wrap around me and I know it's Paul. I'm too
tired to tell him to leave me. As soon as I can talk I'll tell him.

But I feel something else. More arms around me.

Someone is murmuring, "It's okay, it's okay." The air around
me is close and filled with people breathing in my space, my air.
I think everyone has their arms around me. I stop crying with
the surprise of it. And the fact that it feels good.

"Well, isn't this touching," a voice says above us. It has an
English accent.

We break apart and I snap my head up. I look around but
there's no one there.

The room we're in is almost completely empty except for

mounted deer heads, ram heads, antelope heads on the wall. There are coats of arms leaning on wainscoting all around the perimeter of the room, one a lion and a unicorn. An old-fashioned life-sized ornate carriage with closed curtains stands in the corner. A white ram directly above me is talking. I scramble up and look at him.

Little laughs titter around the room.

The ram speaks. "Good lord, you people smell. Did you bathe in fish?"

Ashley huffs out. Her blonde hair is stringy down her back. She has trickles of blood trailing with streams of water down her arms and even her face. Her feet are a mess of red. They look so bad I have to look away again.

I glance at each one of us. We are all the same—a mess of blood and water. The gash in Dylan's forearm is bad. I can't look at it without feeling sick. Paul has a long wound on his forehead that I know was from that subhuman thing in the scuba suit. I look at my hands. They are covered in scratches. A piece of glass sticks up between my forefinger and thumb. I pull it out with a hiss. And then I put my hand on my ear and inhale sharply. Salt water and wounds. Awesome.

That's when I notice that Paul is looking at the bottom of the door. Everyone is. Water is leaking through.

Gretchen suddenly turns to Ashley, eyes flashing. "You left us!"

Ashley shifts on her feet, her face creased in pain. "I came back," she says. "Which you should be thanking me for, by the way." There isn't any fire in her voice, though. None at all.

I think Ashley is having a feeling—which would be a banner day any other day. But this type of feeling I think she's having is revolutionary. I think she feels bad.

Dylan says softly, "Gretch, she saved my life."

Gretchen flips around, "We all did. We all helped each other. Except her." Her voice is shaky and hard. I can see she is close to tears, something I never thought I'd see. Ever. And I realize she's not actually mad at Ashley. She's doing something my

psychology professor mom used to accuse me of all the time—
she's transferring. She's transferring her scared feeling to
something she understands.

Anger. Hurt. Betrayal.

Ashley and Gretchen start going at it again. Both have pale
faces, wide eyes. Both are visibly shaking. Their words are gib-
berish. I can't help but think of alpha monkeys fighting for land.

Something shifts inside of me.

"Stop fighting, you guys," I say quietly.

Ashley and Gretchen keep at it. And, before I can stop myself
I yell it. "STOP FIGHTING."

Everyone looks at me.

Shoot. Now I actually have to say something.

So, I say the first thing that comes to mind. And, surprisingly, it's
true. "We did save each other's lives. But I think—no, I KNOW—
that this House or demon or whatever wants us to think we're alone
in this, and that we have to fight with each other to get out alive.
But . . ." I swallow. I'm in new territory here, not at all sure what I'm
saying. But it feels right. "I kind of believe that in order for any of
us to get out, we *all* have to get out. Like, together . . ."

Everyone has gone quiet. They stare at me, so I keep going.

"Look, we're not even halfway done with this House," I continue. "Every room is going to be something else we have to
face. So I say we make a pact here and now that it's all for one.
Understand? We always come back for each other. Always. We
are all getting out of this alive—I think it's the only way." I stand
up straighter. The pain in my ear stops throbbing for just a
second. "We do this together."

Paul starts nodding. Ashley half-shrugs. Dylan and Gretchen
nod along with Paul. All four move in closer.

Then the ram laughs.

He turns his head to his fellow wall mounts and says in a
mocking voice, "'We do this together.'"

One of the antelopes laughs, too, and says, "Hey, how many
of these stupid kids does it take to screw in a lightbulb?"

The unicorn on the coat of arms snicker-neighs. "I bet it's 0. Because they're all going to die!"

Ashley turns around tiredly. "Yeah, yeah. We're all going to die here. We've heard it already. Really, the *unicorn* can't think of something original?"

The unicorn tries to disengage itself from the coat of arms, saying, "How dare you, girl!" and the lion on the other side says, "Hey. You're going to knock us off."

I snort. Ha. Haaaaaa!!!

This is, quite possibly, the funniest thing I've ever seen or heard.

Gretchen has started to laugh a little and she shakes off Dylan's arm and stands next to Ashley. "Hey Ash, how many unicorns does it take to screw in a lightbulb?"

Ashley turns to Gretchen in stage-like interest, "I don't know, Gretch, how many?"

"They can't. Because they're too stupid to get off a coat of arms!"

This actually isn't that funny. And a person in the outside world would wonder what made a group of people laugh so hard about mocking a unicorn. Even a mean one. Or maybe they'd wonder about a talking unicorn. But we have completely lost it. Completely. Every one of us starts laughing. I feel the laugh start from my toes and it is so hard and hysterical that I double over.

The rams and antelopes and deer start making indignant noises, "Well, I never," and, "You are insulting a UNICORN, Madame," and all of it just makes me laugh harder.

And I start to feel something else, too, coming from the bottom of my feet, moving up my entire body like light and good and water after a desert walk.

Hope.

PAUL

Though this be madness, yet there is method in it.

Violet. Darling Violet. You beautiful creature, you. Yes. Let's stick together.

I am going to marry that girl. High school sweethearts still exist, right? Hell. There was a talking, asshole unicorn trying to attack us—surely our love would last. If she loved me back. I can feel the ghost of her hand in mine and I flex it to try to keep the feeling.

I take a step back and feel water on my ankles. A quick look back and I see that water is now pouring under the door, like someone has stuck a hose right under it and is watering this room. With ocean.

I put my hand on Violet's soft arm and she wipes her eyes and looks at me. She is so pretty I almost forget what I'm going to say. I want to kiss her so bad it hurts. Instead, I point to the door. A sigh goes through her whole body and I feel her slump.

A voice from the other side of the room by the carriage near the door says, "Baptism time!" It comes from a small statue in a bishop-like hat, the figure holding a cross. She points the cross at the door near her. "It seems you've been baptized already, young Crusaders. You may want to go that way, though I know not what adventures lie there." She smiles. "Ah, to be able to martyr myself again."

Gretchen looks back at the door, too, and sighs. She picks up her feet and then looks at Ashley's feet. "We need to bandage up. Anyone know what's next?"

Violet, who is smoothing her hair down, says, "I'm pretty sure we're coming up to a café." She crinkles her nose. "And Benjamin Franklin? Why is that sticking in my head?"

Dylan says, "I think there are cars and shit and then a statue of Bennie right before the café."

Gretchen looks at him sharply but then something drains from her face. "We are going to have to talk, you know."

Dylan just nods and looks away. Blood drips off his arm and he holds it with his other hand. The guy is hurt bad. I feel a sting on my forehead and I remember being cut by the glass from the cases. Ashley's feet look like raw meat. We are all in really bad shape.

"Well. Let's go." Gretchen moves over to Ashley and has her throw her arm around her. Dylan gets on her other side. They start walking, Ashley taking sharp breaths with each step. Violet follows and I bring up the rear. When Violet reaches the carriage, the curtain suddenly slides open and a huge doll looks at us. She has a tattered Victorian dress on and is holding another doll that has no arms. The no-armed doll says "Mama" in a mechanical voice, its mouth not moving, its face fixed. The doll holding it takes it by a leg and smacks it against the carriage wall. The no-armed doll goes quiet and the Victorian doll slides the curtain shut.

Ashley mutters through clenched teeth, "Jesus Christ," and the statue says, "YES! Jesus! I'm coming!"

Gretchen says, "Dear God, save me from your followers," and I swear I see Dylan flinch.

But we are through the door and I'm the last one out, so I close the pocket door.

And find myself in a huge open area at the top of yet another ramp. Big cardboard star shapes populate the air space near us and a half-moon with a wizard on it sits high up and across the enormous room. Fake houses are at the bottom of the room, and I can see the café behind a large wall of glass and the fake houses. No Benjamin Franklin yet. Already I can hear little feet pattering. More dolls. More goddamn dolls.

On our left are more glass cases, and I can already hear chattering in some of them. I flinch and I feel Violet in front of me tense up.

Please no walking guys in old-timey jumpsuits that attack us and try to throw Ashley at a whale. Please. The gash in my forehead hurts just thinking it.

A voice across the way says, "Hi-ho! Welcome to our homes!" It's the wizard and it's waving at us. "I say, could somebody help me down? I'm afraid I don't remember how I got up here. Old age, you see." He chuckles. He mutters something to himself and looks all around the moon he's on, putting a foot down gingerly into air and then bringing it back up. I glance at Violet and throw her a quick smile. She smiles back at me, but it's sad.

None of us answers him. We keep walking, Ashley still breathing in sharply every step. We are accident victims moving toward another accident.

The first glass case we pass has puppets in it, just hanging. When we pass by, they go crazy, bouncing up and down on their strings, chattering their wooden mouths up and down. Some of them get enough momentum to kick the glass. It's totally creepy. One of them laughs and then the rest of them do, too. The Gretchen-Ashley-Dylan triad speeds up and Ashley's pain noises come faster. There is a trail of blood behind them that makes it look like they're dragging a carcass. The drops of blood here and there are probably from Dylan's arm. I watch Violet wince with all three for every step.

At the turn in the ramp is a door with an exit sign above it. When we get there, no one speaks but we stop and are still.

I'm pretty sure they're all waiting for me to try the door. Only, I don't want to try it. I'm totally, 100 percent freaked out by this whole House. But I look at the three in front of me, limping and bloody. Violet next to me being all Violety . . . If this isn't a time for capes, I don't know what is.

I step forward.

The door in front of me has one of those horizontal push latches across it. Above the door and the sign is a cardboard dragon. I mean, it's a cardboard dragon. Who has a cardboard dragon?

I take a step toward the door and hear skittering up above me and see, just in time, the dragon blow fire down at the door. I jump back into Dylan who jumps back, too, dragging Ashley who says, "Feet, feet, fucking hell!"

The dragon, curiously, is still cardboard, but now its snout is smoking. It doesn't move. Just to be sure, I take another step toward the door and the dragon comes to life again and breathes fire on the door. The heat blast scorches my face, like opening the oven to check on a pizza. I squint and see that the door is fused to the frame anyway.

Violet sighs so loud I feel it in my bones. And this makes me sadder than anything I thought possible.

If Violet is losing hope, then we are all done for.

Gretchen looks again at Ashley's feet, her face serious with what I could swear is concern. "Should we carry you?"

Ashley, pale and shaking, grits her teeth and shakes her head. She tries to take another step but whimpers. Gretchen looks at Dylan and with that relationship telepathy I've seen happen before—my mom and dad had it—they seem to decide something. Dylan takes the lead and bends down, picking up Ashley with his butt. She hesitates but then wraps her arms around his neck, her face relaxing.

"We got you, dudette," Dylan says softly.

Right then, more than anything, I wish I was more like Dylan. He sacrifices without thinking, just like my dad used to. Not like me. I think all the time. I'm afraid all the time. A pit opens up in my chest.

Gretchen, her hand on Ashley's back, says, "Let's just make it to the café."

Everyone starts walking.

When I pass the dragon, I flip it off. Then I feel idiotic. That's as tough as I get. Brave in the face of danger, once the danger has already passed.

Part IV

PEOPLE BEGAN DISAPPEARING.

Maxwell Cartwright Jr. was the first to vanish. Locals knew the day he left—the sun shone brighter, the crows disappeared, the laughter of children could be heard again. The pall over the land lifted. Many felt they could breathe better than they had in years, like a film of something had been lifted and they could finally draw air.

But the shadows of the House grew deeper. The sculptures dimmed darker. The lodge sat in silence and the locals knew: stay away from Boulder House.

But as the world became more fixed, more certain, more *rational*, the rumors and legends about the House faded. People noticed the disappearance of a person here or there, of course. But the concern never lasted long. The disappeared were termed "troubled" and "impulsive." Mental illness was blamed or a bad home life, or any number of maladaptations that might make a person vanish. Authorities would ask if the disappeared had wanderlust, a desire to be free. Perhaps the scenery in the wild Wisconsin woods wooed them back to nature, talked them into a more peaceful life, away from the pressures of modern culture. In hindsight, their friends and families would say, there were clues they would run away. They should have known. But maybe the disappeared were happy now. Maybe, finally, they'd found some peace.

Deep in the House, though, deep in the collections, those

who lost Maxwell Cartwright Jr.'s games had not found peace. The disappeared found only pain. Pain and shame and horror. With each passing year, they forgot a little more who they were and why they were there. And in time, their only purpose was to wait for the times they could release some of the indescribable rage they felt, with no recollection of why they felt it. In time, they lost any idea of who they were. In time, they lost all humanity. And when that happened, they forever and always became belongings of Maxwell Cartwright Jr.

Excerpt from p. 134, *The Collections of Maxwell Cartwright Jr.*

GRETCHEN

She did save Dylan's life. And I was a bitch to her. But more, her feet look like a scene from a *Saw* movie. Jesus. So I try to move us all fast enough to get past the shit on the ramp (glass cases again—come on!) and get us to the café. I keep getting glimpses of down below.

We are coming up on this thing that's called "The Rube Goldberg Contraption." It's this huge train, only it's got a chicken and some figure playing the fiddle on it and a moose . . . What the . . . ?

Paul says, looking at my eyebrows, "Ever see those cartoons or *Pee-wee's Big Adventure,* where they put together a contraption to make toast or something? That's what this is. It's like a machine that makes things complicated."

Like my feelings for Dylan. I say out loud, "Like this whole fucking House." Everyone huffs out. Dylan says, "Truth, yo."

We pass by this machine on our right, and as the fiddler starts fiddling, a monkey above him begins to move and dance and make monkey noises. Luckily, everything is behind a huge piece of plastic and doesn't seem to be making moves toward us. Not that I'd trust them as far as I could throw them.

I don't trust anything in this House. I don't trust FULL STOP on a good day. And this is not a good day.

Next is a Hells Angel-looking tuba player whose cheeks puff in and out while the tuba makes a dusty tooting sound. Then some punching gloves tap a chicken that clucks and lays an egg and then the egg seems to hit a moose that kicks something else and it all ends in this cat getting up and stretching and yawning. Despite myself, I am walking slowly past this weird thing, wondering what the hell is going on when the old-fashioned cars on the floor across the way start honking and flashing their lights.

The sound beats my eardrums and I clamp my hands over my ears. And then as abruptly as it starts, it stops. But my jangling nerves don't.

We turn the corner of the ramp and see a house that says ICE CREAM on it. Farther down is the large glass wall and the café behind it. And Benjamin Franklin before the entrance.

I hear the little footsteps. Motherfucking dolls in this motherfucking House, as Dylan would say. I make sure to keep my eyes up so I know if any dolls are coming down on me.

We get to the Benjamin Franklin statue and it snaps its head up. "Hello, travelers. Do remember: Lost time can never be found again. Honesty is the best policy. Tricks and treachery are the practice of fools that don't have brains enough to be honest. Three can keep a secret if two are dead. He who—"

Ashley yells at him, "Shut the fuck up, Benjamin Franklin!"

And Paul says, "Seriously."

Violet says, "Yes, please."

Dylan says, "For real, yo. And Ashley, dudette, that was right in my ear."

And I say, "Hallefuckinglujah."

"Well," Ben Franklin says. But then he shuts up. Ashley grins at me from her perch on Dylan—who is huffing a little since she probably weighs more than he does—and I grin back, but then I remember I hate her so I furrow my eyebrows again and walk into the café.

I hate her, right?

At one end is a fortuneteller like Madame Josefina. This one has brown hair. She says in a soft, beautiful voice, "Come here, darlings. Let me tell you your future."

Violet says, "Eff off!"

I stop and look at her. I say, "Violet!" half-joking. We all laugh a little.

The fortuneteller mumbles, "Needn't be rude, you know. I'd rather not be here either."

But we're all smiling at each other now.

Dylan puts Ashley down in a booth toward the end of the room. Then he runs to the counter that is at the other end of the café and jumps over it, like it's a turnstile. Kid is talented that way. How does he have the energy?

He dips down below and then pops up, his hands full of sandwiches. "'Wiches Bitches!" He yells and I swear to god we all run at him like we're being chased. Except for Ashley who yells, "I want all of them!"

He starts throwing them at us and everyone catches theirs except Violet who drops it and says, "Oh, shoot," but she's laughing and I'm laughing, and for the first time since I stepped into the Wheel House room, I don't feel insane.

Dylan grabs some sodas from a mini fridge behind him and we each take one then go to Ashley in the booth. Dylan and I cram on the other side of Ashley, and Paul and Violet sit across from each other at a table, every once in a while looking up at each other in this gross sickening way that makes me roll my eyes. I share a look with Ashley and she snorts.

Jesus. They should just do it already.

I clear my throat.

No one talks for a full five minutes. The sandwich I'm eating is the best sandwich I've ever eaten in my entire life. My. Entire. Life.

When we're done, I look at Ashley and her pale face. I notice blood dripping down the booth seat. I notice blood on the table from Dylan's arm. Paul's head isn't bleeding anymore, though, and Violet's ear looks mangled and red and only half there, but not oozy.

Ashley is by far the worst. I say, "How are they?" She shrugs.

Then looks up and smiles at me, her eyes huge and her face white as shit. "My pedicurist will have her work cut out for her."

It's kind of an asshole thing to say. She can actually say that and mean it.

But she has sweat beading on her upper lip and I can tell she is in mega pain. And I have to give the girl props for not complaining. Not once. I say, "We need to do something with those."

She hesitates and inhales, then nods. I get up, searching for something to start bandaging people up with. For some reason, I'm the least hurt of all of us. Scrapes here and there, but nothing serious.

I duck behind the café counter and walk into the kitchen. It smells like every industrial kitchen ever. I open steel cupboards and drawers and come up with nothing.

And then, in the corner, I spot a huge box with a red cross on it.

Bingo.

I grab it and some clean towels I see in one of the drawers and come back out.

I throw two towels to Violet and Paul and put the first aid box on their table. I grab a huge tube of antiseptic and three towels and turn to Dylan.

Dylan points at Ashley. "Do the dudette first. I stopped bleeding and I can do the salve myself." He grabs the tube, squirts a big glob on his hand and then rubs it into his puncture wound, making blood trickle out again. I wince and my stomach turns.

I just wanted to be a clothing designer. I'm not ready for war.

He grabs a towel and wraps it around his forearm. I swallow down my ick and go to him, tying the cloth tight. Then I go to the other side of the booth to Ashley. I pull up a chair and pull one of her feet toward me, soft. I don't know where to put my hands. Everywhere I touch there is blood.

I open a water bottle and pour it on her feet, trying to wipe around obvious glass pieces so I can get a sense for what I'm dealing with here. Oh, goddess, it's gross.

Ashley is shaking but she goes for a smile. "No glass slippers for me, huh?"

There are at least five glass pieces per foot that I need to take out. And who knows how many that I can't see. This is bad. I need to pick these out fast and I can't have her kicking me or we'll never get done.

I look her hard in the eye, "I have to get this glass out." She swallows and nods. "This is going to suck ass, Ashley. You have to try not to kick me, okay?" She nods again and sets her mouth.

I exhale slowly and point at the first large chunk of many.

"On the count of three, Ash. One—" and then I yank it out. She howls and I smile grimly. "That always works," I say.

She shoots me a shaky smile back. "Asshole." But the way she says it makes me feel warm all over.

ASHLEY

Gretchen is touching my feet.

Actually, Gretchen is massacring my feet.

"FUUUUCCKKK!" I yell as she yanks the second to last asshole piece of glass from my left foot.

"Hold still," she hisses and puts the cool antibiotic cream on the latest wound when it stops bleeding.

In movies, this is supposed to be romantic. But it actually hurts like a motherfucker.

"Last one," she says and before I can say anything, she yanks it out. I grunt. Actually, I make this "grrrrr" sound I didn't know I was capable of producing. Like an animal.

Pain. Everyone is an animal when it comes to pain.

Gretchen wraps my foot in mountains of gauze and tape, then wraps a towel in a complicated bootie shape. Then she tapes it up like the other foot so now I have towel-boot shoes.

Hot.

I try my new shoes out, stepping out of the booth slowly. It hurts—there's probably a ton of glass still in there—but it's a fuckton better. I can actually walk. I grab some leftover tape and put it in my bra since my skirt doesn't have pockets. Because why would I do myself any favors and wear something that wasn't just a teen guy's wet dream? Note to self: when I get out of this, comfortable shoes and things with pockets. Hell, I might even go full-on camo and carry a knife on my belt. Maybe I should butch it up. Seems way more practical.

"Where'd you learn to do something like this?" I ask Gretchen, who is finally getting color back in her face.

Gretchen shrugs as she puts stuff away. She mumbles, "I don't know." And then she clears her throat and says louder. "I make clothes."

I want to know. I want to know about her clothes that I secretly envy though I would never in a million years tell her. I want to thank her in a real way for fixing my feet and not going crazy here. I want to do all those things.

Instead, the air starts vibrating.

All of us stand up and move toward each other.

And then with a POP, the sonuvabitch demon-thingy is in front of us, doing that weird streaky thing and twirling his goddamn cane. The burning egg stench makes my nose twitch.

"Kidssssss," he says, hissing so much it actually hurts my eardrums. "What do you think of the House so far? I trust it's treating you like proper guests?"

He smiles and his teeth are fang-y, his eyes are TWIRLING red. What the hell?

I swallow and lean into the whole group. I would kill for a gun right now. Or that knife on a belt.

Gretchen, her voice shaking, says, "What do you want from us? Why won't you let us out of here?"

Violet starts to cry. I'm two seconds away from that.

I'd take a whale and a squid any day over this asshole.

He suddenly stops walking and it feels like time stops. He claps his hands like a gleeful kid. "What spirit you've shown! What . . . togetherness." He winks. "However, I just wonder . . ." He puts the cane up against his mouth like he's thinking. "I just wonder how well my darling Five know each other." He wiggles his eyebrows.

He twirls his cane again and begins walking around us. He clears his throat, then stands still like he's at an imaginary podium giving a lecture. "I have chosen you for this game for very particular reasons. Because you all have some delicious tidbits about yourselves, don't you? Interests, doings, the like, that you've perhaps never shared before?"

Ice shards poke down my spine. Oh shitball fuck.

He looks at Gretchen. "For instance!" He points his cane at her. "I know Gretchen here is terribly embarrassed of her living situation. Why is that, Gretchen, dear?"

I feel Gretchen's body stiffen. He goes on. "Why is it you make your own clothes? Why are you so darn *different?*" He cocks his head like he's trying hard to think of why.

I see an actual sweat bead on her forehead. He cackles. "Shall I tell? Shall I tell them all that your daddy had an affair with a younger woman? That he has a new family now—new, better children? Shall I tell them that he has forgotten you so much that he has forgotten to send money, and you are therefore on . . ." He stops and looks at us, widening his eyes. "Food stamps? You can't even afford food. You are a *taker,* as they say. A mooch. A drain on the American people. I believe you are what they call trailer trash? Tsk tsk. And you seem so independent. Ah well. "

Gretchen shudders and I feel her swallow.

Oh God. She's on food stamps. And how many times have I . . .

Dylan says, "Listen, you demon sonuvabitch—"

But the thing points his cane at him. "Yes, let's talk about YOU, *Dylan!*" Dylan shuts right up and takes a step back.

"Or should I say, John?" Gretchen's bitch brows furrow at that. Douchemunch demon guy goes on. "Yes, Ms. Gretchen, did you know your darling boy, Mr. Skater-man, takes-you-on-dates-with-couch-change anarchist non-conforming punk guy is actually John Luke Desmond, member of the Holy Evangelical Christ Church?"

Gretchen takes a step back. Dylan or . . . John? . . . or whatever says, "Gretch—"

But the demon keeps going: "Our John here goes to church like a good boy three times a week. His wonderful parents— yes, his parents are still together—Mr. and Mrs. Desmond have taken John and his sister, Ruth, to many different vacation spots. They're quite well-to-do, you see. They've even been in here, though they decided it was a bit dark for their beliefs. I haven't the faintest idea why." He looks around like he's all innocent. "Next time, they'll be going to the Creation Museum in Kentucky." He winks at Dylan. Or John. Or whatever his name is. And, suddenly, sweat starts down my spine. If he's telling their secrets . . .

"It appears you CAN'T trust any men, dearest Gretchen. They're all just like your dad." He winks at her. "John here is not from a broken, alcoholic home like he's told you. He's from a Bible-thumping, holy-rolling, food-stamp-hating, no-fornication, women-in-their-place, promise-keeper kind of home."

Gretchen's expression is so vulnerable, I have to look away. She looks like she is going to pass out.

The sweat has pooled in my bra by the tape. Please tell me he's done.

Then he trains his eyes on me.

DYLAN

My baby won't look at me.

The whole world just dropped out from under my feet. My sun, moon, stars. Gretchen won't look at me. I barely hear what the demon dude says after I see the look on Gretchen's face.

But the asstroll stares at Ashley, taking a nice long break from talking, to let everything sink in. Gretchen sits down. I move toward her, but she puts up her hand and I know this gesture. It's the heartbreak gesture. *My* heartbreak. The don't-touch-me gesture.

Babe is hurt. Because of me. I can't breathe.

There are reasons, I want to shout. *There are reasons why,* I think-scream.

But now the demon dude is talking again. He's clocking Ashley. I get the game now, too late. I get the game, now that I'm destroyed. The game is "Secret secret, who's got a secret." Ashley has started shaking.

I'm expecting a long windup, the way he tortured Gretch and me. But instead, the dude points his cane at Ashley and says, "She's gay!"

We all flip our heads to Ashley. She takes a step back on her towel boots.

The demon walks around and giggles. "Now, that is hardly scandalous in this day and age. But consider this, peer court! Consider that Ashley came here specifically to meet an Internet paramour for some, what sexual education manuals call, 'heavy petting.'"

He lifts one eyebrow and puts a finger to his creepy shark mouth. "Our Ashley enjoys leading on these poor girls—girls who think she may be the one, the sweetheart of their hearts—and using and discarding them like so many Gucci purses."

He stops again. "'But,' you might say, 'while this is not exemplary, kind behavior, certainly it is not horrifying.' My dears, you would be wrong. Ashley here follows her daddy dearest soon-to-be senator's stance in public: Down with the gays. Marriage between one man and one woman. Homosexuality is a sin for depraved monsters and godless heathens. And all that delicious folderol that religion has devised to separate humans. Sound familiar, John?"

He winks at me. I wince. That sonuvabitch. I look to Gretchen again but she has her head in her hands now. *I don't believe that, Gretch. Believe me. Believe in me.*

Demon dude takes another lap and looks at Paul. Who physically ducks.

But he whips his head around to Ashley again and says, waving his hand lazily, "Oh, and she's in love with Gretchen here."

My body jerks. Whaaaaa???

"Paul!" says the demon dude. Paul tries to speak, "I don't care what you have to—" But the demon interrupts him.

"Undoubtedly you don't care. You don't care at all that you are quite the popular boy at River Red High School in the quaint town of Whispering Bluffs, Wisconsin. Quite the basketball player, quite the laaaaadies' man. Tell me, Paul, does everyone know that you and your mom take SCA classes? Enact some old Renaissance Faire scenes?" He puts his hand to one side of his mouth and says, "Brings out ye olde jerkin, what what." He winks at me and then says, "Is that called LARPing, Paul? I am so far behind the terms these days."

I blink. SCA? And as if he's reading my mind, the freak show demon says, "Oh, for those of you who don't know, it's the Society of Creative Anachronism. Dressing up. And LARPing is Live Action Role Playing."

He bends down near us and we all back up. He stage whispers, "It's role-playing for, what you may say in this day and age, *dorks*. You know. For those too cowardly to live in the real world."

He bounds up. "Paul here looks dashing with a sword. And tights. Violet, darling, wouldn't you love to see Paul's sword?"

Blood has started rushing to Paul's face, but it's Violet's face that keeps me looking. She looks pure-D terrified. Terrified with a capital T-E-R-R.

Girl turns and tries to sprint toward Ben Franklin. She tries to actually run. Holy shit. But demon dude appears in front of her, a streak that turns solid. She yelps, skids to a stop, then falls backward. She looks up at him. He slams his cane down right between her legs.

"But I think our Violet here has the most delicious secret, don't you, Violet?"

She has started crying and whispers, "Please don't . . ."

Despite myself, I am leaning forward.

Demon dude says, "Ashley, you and Ms. Violet here have some things in common. Like, partaking in the occasional . . . sensual leisure activities."

I see Paul take a step closer.

He goes on. "See, our Violet here is having an affair, too. But only with one person, unlike you, Ashley. Our Violet here seems to attract the *older man*. In this case, the older *married* man." He stops and puts a finger on his chin. "Tell me, Violet, because I forget: does Mr. Rhinehart have any children?"

The silence falls like a predator, eating us up.

VIOLET

When I learned to ride my bike, my dad wouldn't let me have training wheels. He said it would "toughen me up," but he said it in shrink talk. As in, "teach her autonomy, victory through perseverance, which will grow into a healthy sense of self." What it gave me was a lot of scraped knees.

I take that back. It did do all those things. I remember sticking my tongue out and pedaling pedaling pedaling, my hands wobbling on the handlebars, rough tread of the grips scraping along my palms, the fishtailing of the back wheel. I remember doing this and falling down over and over until I finally did do it. I learned how to ride that ever-loving bike. By myself. And though I would never say it to my dad, he was right. I'm glad that's the way I learned.

But something that I wouldn't ever tell anyone—something that I remember more than anything else, even more than the victory of winning the Battle of the Bike—is the feeling of falling. That moment when you know you no longer have control. The wobble of the handlebars gets bigger and bigger, swings wider and wider, and pretty soon you can't get a fix on what's in front of you. Just green and pavement and then the unmoored feel of falling. That free float for a few tiny, interminable seconds, when you are neither here nor there, fish nor fowl, as my gran would say. You are no one. You are alone. Unloved. Unanchored. Unable to breathe. Doomed.

I am falling.

I hear Paul from far away say, "Violet?" His face ashen, his brown eyes—beautiful, kind, forgiving, pleading?—are set in an expression of disbelief. Betrayal.

And then I see it. What I was afraid of most. What has kept me up at night. What I feel for myself, most days.

Disgust.

I take in a huge breath, gasping like a fish flopping on the shore. Oceanless. I realize I have forgotten to breathe.

Dylan, or John, or whatever his name is, stares at me and lets out a whoosh of air. Ashley says "fuuuuuck" so softly I can barely hear it. Gretchen just stares wide-eyed at me. Paul hasn't moved.

The House or the Demon or My Death or whatever-it-is waits a beat and then twirls his cane around. My body shakes and my teeth chatter. But it's like it's happening to someone else. I can't feel my lips.

He brushes his hands together like he's wiping something off and takes a big breath. He looks around the room and puts his hands on his hips. "Well," he says. "Now that you know who all of you really are, what rotten things lie underneath, would you like to stay together or try to get through my game alone?"

I think of Paul's look of disgust. Dylan's lies to Gretchen for years. Ashley's hypocrisy. How they all must hate me now. I know I hate myself.

Alone is better. Alone is what I deserve.

So before anyone else can talk, I take a final look around at the people I had just started to consider my friends. I look to the boy I think I could've fallen in love with. And I close my eyes as the tears come.

I say: "Alone."

Faster than I thought possible, the demon claps his hands hard and a flash of light spreads through the room, like a nuclear blast.

My life explodes.

ASHLEY

Jesus. H. Christ. Wherever I am reeks.

After the white flash, I land on my stomach somewhere. I feel carpet under my arms, smelling of years of god-knows-what tramping through here. Probably kid hork and gum and . . . Jesus. I stand up as fast as my bandaged feet will let me. I wince as my weight settles on them, my hands out for balance. Thank god Gretchen bandaged these puppies well.

Gretchen.

I swallow. Close my eyes. Try to fight the burning shame bugs running up and down my spine. Fuck.

Gretchen.

"What are you doing here?" The voice is loud and takes up the whole room.

I jump and step back.

I'm in a completely red room. A red bench runs the length of the room behind me, and in front of me: a stern-looking, ancient-y Chinese man fronting a huge kettle drum.

I take a look around. Besides the display of instruments and statues in front of me, I'm alone.

For a minute I marvel about Violet. I can't help it, I feel for this girl. The look on her face . . . And goddamn Rhinehart? I mean, that's really bad. But . . . not because of her. Rhinehart's a fucking predator, clearly. I could have told her that the minute I met him.

Violet was right: alone is better, though. Isn't this what I wanted? Except how come it doesn't feel good?

To my right, from the doorway, I hear little footsteps, the shush-shush of feet on carpet. Adrenaline spikes through me. Dolls. It's got to be those asshole dolls.

Except what walks in is not a doll. It's a little figure, like a gnome, only not goofy-looking. He is about thigh height and he's got a beard and a green hat that's long and pointed. Maybe a dwarf? He's a creature I don't really understand. In his hands, he holds a mask. He stares down at it, a puzzled look on his face.

He stops near me and looks up, but he barely pays attention to me. He looks down at his mask again, twisting it left and right in his hands. He holds it up to his face and looks through it.

And then he puts it on.

The mask conforms to his face, wrapping around his head like a living thing. The face of it is a big smile, like a cartoon smile or that smiling theater mask thingy. His eyes are dead. He looks up at me again. And then runs out of the room.

From the door he came in, another figure enters, this time my height. He has a trumpet or something in his mouth and he wears a full jumpsuit like a clown, with polka dots and billowy legs and arms. But the colors are muted and he's got no face paint, so he's not exactly clown-y. He's like a serious clown or something. His hat is a triangle and his hair sticks up around the brim. He plays a muted melody, haunting and lonely. Low notes, slow, dissonant. My body reacts to it without my permission. My shoulders slump. My head aches. Another dwarf person walks by his side, looking up at him. This dwarf has a mask on, too—his is stuck in a sad face. He trains his eyes, if you can call them that, on me. Then he looks back up at the trumpet player.

They walk by me without saying a word. Without acknowledging my presence at all. I feel tears on my cheeks.

Alone.

I jump when the guy in front of the kettle drum says again, "What are you doing here?"

I wipe my face. Clear my throat. I can do something about

this feeling. I can do something. I may not be the best person in the world, but I can do shit.

"Have you seen my friends?" I ask, hoping against hope this is a nice ancient-y Chinese man with a kettle drum.

He throws a drum mallet at me. I duck just in time.

NOT a nice ancient-y Chinese man.

He laughs an evil laugh. "Friends? You don't have friends. No one wants to be with you now. Now that they know. Especially her."

Crying is for the weak, I tell myself. Crying is for people with no self-control. Just like my dad always says.

But I feel tears spring to my eyes again anyway.

Because asswipe kettle drum guy is right. She does hate me. And asswipe demon guy was right, too. I am in love with her. All those days looking forward to her, not to make fun of her. To see her. So stupid. Loving someone straight, someone who hates me. Fuck.

I suck in a breath and muster anger. "Go back to your own country!"

He looks confused. "I am in my own country."

And then I full-on start crying. I move backward, sit on the bench behind me, put my face in my hands, and let my whole body shake.

"You've made her cry," says a stern female voice. I look up, wiping my nose. A golden figure, a small statuette in flowing robes, on one side of the kettle drum guy is talking. "Shame on you."

The man sniffs and gestures with his one remaining drum mallet. "She deserves it." Asshole.

The woman says, "Tsk Tsk. Really. Any more than anyone else?"

"Well," he says. "She's mean. And racist."

I hiccup and say to the woman. "He's right. I AM mean. And I'm a hypocrite. And I'm an asshole. I'm probably more than a little racist and if I'm honest I've always thought that poor people are just stupid and lazy and deserve to be poor." My voice has turned into a whine and I'm doing that hiccup sob thing where I can't catch my breath. I think of all the times I've made someone's life hell. And my dad, my stupid dad—what kind of an asshole is he? To care if someone is gay or not? The shit he's said about immigrants, about anyone not white. Even I know it's bullshit. And to be mean to people who don't have money? Like Gretchen. Who is on food stamps. Fuck. She's on food stamps and how many times have I . . .

And it hits me. I am my dad. I am exactly what my family wants me to be. A hypocrite asshole. I don't even know who I am underneath everything.

And now I'm in this goddamn House with bandages on my feet and awful hair and my secret is out to everyone and the girl I'm in love with is straight and hates me and I'm talking to a statuette and a mannequin with a kettle drum.

Karma's a bitch.

"Listen, little girl. You have time, you know. You are young," the nice woman statuette says. "This too shall pass. Nothing is as dire as you think it is—time wipes away all. But you must get out."

I think about that for a minute. Here, I don't have time. Here, I'm going to die. Probably at the tiny hands of a doll. Alone.

I sit up straighter. Why *am* I alone all of a sudden? Why did that demon asshole tell everyone all our secrets?

And then it dawns on me: Because we were sticking together. Because we were getting along. We were surviving together. He basically tried to get us to abandon each other. This is the game. It must be. And he's winning.

Demon douche guy is afraid of us sticking together. Violet guessed it. She guessed it early on and the douche guy is nervous.

Which probably means that Paul, Gretchen, Dylan, and Violet are out there somewhere, each in separate rooms, all by themselves, too.

And maybe they're in rooms that don't just have some snarky kettle drum guy making them feel bad about themselves. Most of this House wants to eat us alive.

That's when I hear glass break somewhere in the House, somewhere not in the room with me.

Something's gotten out.

GRETCHEN

I'm on my back and all I can see is blue around me. A blue, plush ceiling, like from the 1700s. Blue velvet walls. Even the carpet I'm on—which smells totally gross—is lush and blue. I stand up and take a look in front of me. Behind a knee-high, ornate wall stand cellos, violins, and cymbals; there's a white plush ceiling, like the upholstery of a super-swank couch, candelabras everywhere, blue velvet chairs that look more expensive than anything I've ever owned. The exact opposite of my home. My shitty duplex on the bottom, with the family with six kids up above, little feet and big feet constantly stomping at all hours of the night. The barking little mongrel of a dog. No rest for the wicked, I guess. I must be pretty wicked.

And here I am, stuck in a room made for rich people.

I look to my left and start—I think I've seen a person, but it's just me in the mirror. My bleach blonde hair is lit from above. It should make me look angelic, really, that kind of lighting. But I just look tired. I have bags under my eyes. My roots are showing, dark and dingy near the rest of my hair. My skin looks gray. I look thirty years older than I am. The words jump in my mind faster than I can squash them down, faster than my excuses and my lies to myself.

I look like trailer trash.

Actually, a trailer would probably be nicer than our shithole home.

I surprise myself with a sharp bark of a laugh. Well. There

you have it. The truth. I feel my muscles relax, I feel the furrow between my brows unfurrow. I am who I am. My dad didn't want me, didn't think I was worth staying for or even getting to know. He knew already. He knew. No use in trying so hard. I can just let go now, get knocked up, work at Walmart for no pay like my mom. I should probably start smoking. My teeth are too straight, too white. Dylan is always commenting on them.

Dylan.

John.

I sit straight down on the floor, like I'm a puppet whose master has found something else to play with. My strings cut, on my own now.

Dylan.

I don't feel anything though, not really. Just a draining, like someone pulled a stopper and all the feeling is leaking out. An emptying. I can stop pretending to be in love with him, too. Because as long as I'm being honest, I can, well, be honest— that I loved him at first because he was different. Because he was weird and unique and he fit who I was trying to be. And now he's like a brother to me because we've been dancing this dance so long. We fit each other's lies. But I'm not in love with him anymore. Whoever he is.

Another laugh barks out of me, comes from deep inside my stomach. Turns out, Dylan's outclassed me by a million. That church the devil-man mentioned is for evangelical *rich* people. Dylan, my alt-'80s-band-T-shirt-wearing eyeliner-sporting freak of a boyfriend is an evangelical rich dude.

He and my dad can have lunch. Talk about how worthless I am.

Music starts out of nowhere. A waltz, but fast and lively, and I realize it's coming from the instruments in front of me. Happy, fast, lively music in the rich, velvety room. Probably something like Ashley's room.

Ashley. What the . . . ? I mean, kind of flattering, totally confusing, a bit of a turn-on, as long as I'm being honest, but holy shit. And then I think of all of them. Paul, Dylan, Ashley . . .

Violet. Fucking Violet! Who knew? I start giggling. Good god, what a bunch of freaks we are. Freaks thrown together.

Freaks who fought together.

And then I stop laughing right away. *They* all fit together. Not like me. Not like me and my EBT card, my rags for clothes.

I can't find my hard edges. I can't find anything. I'm empty.

I can let this House kill me now. I look around the room and for once there is nothing around that could possibly harm me. Unless violins can walk . . .

Violet was right to pick being alone.

I take a last look at my face in the mirror. Tired, baggy eyes— my future—looks back at me.

Time to put an end to that. Time to find out what this House can do. If this House can do what it has promised to do since the Wheel House wheel started turning.

I walk out of the rich room where I don't belong.

DYLAN

After the white light blast that the douchetroll somehow made with his hands, the next thing I know, I hit the ground hard on my back on pavement or cobblestone or something boxy and ouch-y. My head bounces off the ground and I grunt from the impact.

Fuck-a-doodle-doo.

I'm in some place that looks like the Streets of Yore, only different. There's an old-timey organ and a storefront that says DELIVERY on it, where a horse stands attached to a wagon. It stomps its foot.

Oh, God. Another horse. Nice horsey.

I don't remember this part of the House at all. I have no idea where I am. Or where anyone else is. Including Gretch.

My heart breaks in a million pieces when I think of the look on her face. If I shake my feet I'll hear the glass shards of my heart, I swear. My Gretchen.

Where is she? Where is anyone? We should not be alone. We should not. No matter what. Violet chose wrong.

Holy shit. Violet. With Rhinefart? Poor girl.

"You're alone, alone John Luke," a voice says. The hairs on the back of my neck stand up. The voice is whiney and uber creepy, like that Skeksis from *The Dark Crystal*, an old film Gretch and I watched a million times together.

I whip my head around and see the horse stomp again. Cobblestone, wagon, organ, jester in glass case, fake leg sitting in a storefront . . .

I flip my head around to the jester, who is almost exactly my height. It laughs all of a sudden. "Ha! It's me who is talking, John Luke! It's me, it's me!"

The jester is in a green and red stripy outfit with yellow mixed in. His hat curves toward his face and there are bells all around it that jingle as he talks. His chin is mega-huge and so is his nose. But his eyes, yo. His eyes are fucking nutso. Like, Courtney Love nuts.

He smashes himself up against the case. "Let us out, John Luke. Let us out, yes? We are like you, we are like you." His nose squeaks against the glass.

I back up. "Dude, what are you talking about?"

He does a little jig in his case. "We dance. We dance for our supper."

I shake my head. "Dude. I don't dance. And I'm not, like, plural."

The guy stops and cocks his head like a curious dog. "Are you not? Are you not, John Luke Dylan?"

I wince. Anger shoots through me. Who is this little jester guy? Who is this guy to tell me what's what?

"I'm NOTHING like you." I practically scream at him. "I'm not plural, I'm not two-faced. I *had* to lie. I had to lie to everyone. Because I'm not John Luke. I'm not John. I am Dylan. My parents would never understand. Gretch wouldn't have understood either. I had to lie. I had to lie to make everybody feel better."

The jester laughs. "John Luke Dylan doesn't belong anywhere. You don't belong. No one loves you, no one loves you. You are a freak, like me," he says and then starts dancing, kicking his legs back and forth. "Freaky Dylan Freaky John. Freaky Dylan Freaky John. You don't belong anywhere. You don't belong. You don't belong. Freaky freaky freaky freaky."

"Fuck you!" I yell and back all the way up. I hear the horse whinny. I try to run, but I don't know where to go. I start down the hall one way, but I don't remember this part of the House, so I don't know where it goes. Gretch would know. Gretch would just make a decision. But I can't. I don't know which way to go.

I stop in the middle of the hall in front of the jester, who is now dancing around in a circle in the glass case. Dancing to the song he made about me.

I put my hands over my ears and back up against the wall, sliding down. I can feel the wet down my face and the empty in my insides. No Gretch, no Ashley, no Violet—poor Violet, all alone, all alone—no Paul, no one to help me find my way.

And then the jester stops and says, "Oh. We know how to get out." He head-butts the glass and shards fly at me.

PAUL

Violet.

All I can think of is Violet . . . with that asshole of a teacher? With a TEACHER? With THAT TEACHER? I shudder at the thought of that jerk touching her. How did she stand it?

She said "alone." She chose alone. She didn't choose me.

I'm not sure where I am, some room that is all red, with ornate mirrors and instruments and lanterns and chairs and a carriage and two stuffed saber-toothed tigers in front of me. Music starts up out of nowhere and I jump.

The instruments in front of me are playing by themselves. I think I see one of the tigers twitch, but the light is low so I hope to God I am dreaming it.

Good god. John. Dylan. Gretchen. Violet. Even Ashley. Where are they? Shame spirals through me. They know now. Now they know. I tried so hard to pretend to be someone different.

And she chose "alone." Probably because I'm a total and utter dork. My throat lumps up. Soon I'll be a crying dork. Who has no courage. That's about right.

The music pauses and I hear someone or something clear their throat. I look around and there's no one. The throat clears again, followed by a titter.

Then I look down. It's a mini-horse/centaur thingy. Actually, two of them. One of them looks like he's half-sea-captain like the ones from the whale room and half-horse, and the other one looks like she's half-19th-century-hooker/half-horse. They barely reach my knees. I say, before I can help myself, "May I help you?" And then I think, *They'll bite your kneecaps off.* I back up just a bit.

The man centaur turns to the hooker. "What a polite young man. Nowadays, more young men should be polite like him." He stands up straighter and puts a hand inside the jacket of his uniform, like he's posing for a picture. "I believe you may be of help, son. We are wondering if you can kindly show us the way to the carousel? It appears that the young lady and I," he pauses and winks at the hooker who giggles and stomps a hoof, "have gotten distracted," more titters from the woman, "on our way there." He suddenly looks serious. "They need reinforcements, you know. The angels are ruthless."

I feel my face scrunch up in confusion. I don't even know where to start. "The angels?"

The horse/man snorts and his face turns red. "Indeed! The dirty rotten bastards." He looks at the woman and says, "Pardon my French, Millie." But her eyes blaze and she rears up on her hind legs, then puts her hooves down.

"You bet them angels ain't no good. Right murderers, they are," she says. I can't place the accent. It's like American cockney, if that's a thing.

The man-horse says, "I'm Captain Tidbittles and this is Millie. Now, I have heard tell you have a sword? If this is the case," Captain Tidbittles moves forward and lowers his voice, "I'd be beholden to you for your whole life, sir, if you would but lend it to me to fight this good fight."

Now it's my turn for my face to go red. "Where did you hear I have a sword?"

Captain Tidbittles takes a step back with his four hooves. "Pardon me. I meant no disrespect. Scuttlebutt around here says you carry a sword? And I say to myself, I say, 'Well, that must be a brave man, that. Carrying a sword around, ready to help people out.'" He looks at me and winks. "Help a captain out, in particular."

Millie snorts. "You was helping me out with your sword earlier, wasn't you, Cap'n?"

The two break out in giggles that sound like whinnies and snorts combined. But I feel like the weight of the world is on my shoulders.

"I wish I could help you out, man. But I don't have a sword." I swallow and look up. "I pretend. I playact. I pretend at everything. I pretend I'm brave."

And then I add, "But I'm not."

The captain looks to Millie and she opens her eyes wide and then looks away. He turns back to me. "Well. I apologize. You must not be the young man everyone is talking about. The one who helped stave off the beasts of the ocean and the small beasts of the doll variety. Very well. Millie and I shall have to face the angels with just our intrepid will and our hearts." He stands up tall again. "Which are mighty, I might add."

They start walking (trotting?) away and then for some reason, I can't quit talking. "See, my dad died when I was little and I saw it happen. I couldn't do anything. And ever since, I've been pretending, you see. I've just been pretending that I know what I'm doing. And I don't know who I'm supposed to be, you know? I feel scared all the time. I can't save anyone though. I can't even . . ." I choke on the words, but it doesn't matter because the captain and Millie have trotted away through the door, looking back at me with slightly alarmed looks.

I sit down against the wall and put my head on my knees, letting tears drip down my nose. My mom will miss me. She'll have lost a husband and now a son, too. And I'll never know what it's like to kiss Violet.

Violet. What would she think of me now?

What do I think of her?

But who am I to judge? I talk a big game, but in real life, I'm just a scared little 8-year-old boy who misses his dad. It seems I am only myself when I'm dressing up like someone else.

Violet would do better without me. Rhinehart though? But

then the thought runs through my head, thoughts my mom talked about with me over and over. The minute I hit puberty, she sat me down to talk about two big things: trying to survive in a racist world, and how to treat women and girls. She made me repeat two phrases when it came to the girls' part: consent is key; consent always. Used to embarrass the shit out of me. Like I'd have to be told not to violate a girl who is passed out. But she also talked about power and how shitty people abuse it. And DING DING DING—this is exactly the type of situation she meant. Rhinehart is a goddamn adult. Like, an adult TEACHER. There's a power dynamic there for fuck's sake. Anger shoots through me. Yeah. Not right. He took advantage. He took advantage of Violet. Kindhearted, sweet, tender Violet. He took advantage of her.

That asshole. That motherfucking asshole.

Suddenly, I've got to find Violet. Even if she hates me, even if she thinks I'm too dorky to be with. Because maybe she thinks it's her fault or something. And that's not right. I may not know how I'm supposed to be in the world, but I do know that. I do know that.

My mom's and my favorite Shakespeare line makes me breathe in deeply and sit up straighter. It's time for me to screw my courage to the sticking place.

Oh, yes. Time to find Violet.

I wipe my eyes and my nose, getting ready to stand up. The music has stopped. I stick my hands on the floor and prepare to get out of the room. And then I look up.

Right into the eyes of a tiger.

Another tiger stands right behind him. Low growls ripple through their throats.

They are so close; I can feel their breath huffing on my face.

"Oh, shit," I say.

VIOLET

A bunch of saints look down on me. The saint directly above me says, "Well. I guess we'll just let the sinners have the run of the place then."

One next to her says, "Now, dear, we must have mercy, you know. Even for the lowliest of the low. The worst of the worst. Murderers, rapists, pedophiles, and even her."

Before I can stop myself, I say, "Hey! What do you mean, 'even her'?" The saint looks down at me, almost kindly.

"You're so awful, you see." The other saints, about ten in all, nod their heads in agreement.

I look around me. I'm in a blue room, gold trim everywhere. I'm lying on blue carpet that's flattened in some places. Saints ring around the top of the room. They are dressed in big bishop's hats, with staffs. They look down on me. Literally.

But then an unexpected emotion shoots through me. Anger. Not guilt, not sadness or shame, not anything but anger. It feels good. This must be what Gretchen and Ashley feel all the time.

"You guys . . . you," I say. "Eff you!"

The saints laugh. One guffaws like a donkey braying. Really. It's unbecoming.

A saint says, "Oh, dear. You haven't any idea, have you? Well. That's just as well. You should probably grovel for any sort of attention you can get. You are just you, after all. It's no wonder you had relations with that . . . horrible man."

I hear one saint say, "Thank the good Lord above I swore off men."

She does have a point. But still.

"Listen, you," I say. "I'm not proud of what I have done. But he was . . . I didn't want to hurt his feelings." Even as I say it, I cringe.

I was right to choose alone. The look on Paul's face flashes through my mind and tears form in my eyes. Alone. Like I should be.

Time to be honest. I didn't want to hurt Mr. Rhinehart's feelings. But I also liked the attention. I liked that I was chosen. He chose *me*. No one chooses me. I'm blank, I'm boring, I'm a Forever 21 outfit. He thought I was special.

And now no one else will. Paul won't.

I'm a whore. An attention-seeking, teacher-boffing whore. Shame spirals through me like a unicorn horn. Deep and painful and sharp.

"I need to go now," I say to no one and everyone. Better than sitting in this room alone. I will not cry I will not cry I will not cry in front of these jerky saints.

One of them says what I'm pushing down in my mind.

"Do you really think it matters if you live or die? Do you think anyone will really care if you don't exist anymore?"

My heart sinks to my shoes and I close my eyes. Now tears do escape. "No," I whisper. "No, I don't."

The saint sniffs. "Well, you're right. You might as well stay here."

But then, through my sniffles and the loud voices in my head, I hear a roar. Like the roar of a lion or tiger. And a boy's voice yelling, "GOOD TIGER!"

My heart starts pumping and adrenaline shoots through me.

That was Paul's voice.

Paul.

No time to even wipe my eyes. He's in trouble. And dang it if I'm going to let that stand.

Without thinking, I sprint out of the room.

GRETCHEN

When I hear the glass breaking, the tiger roar, and a boy yelling, I don't even think, I just run. I run through a door that turns into a corridor, and then I hear some sort of heavy drumming start up. I follow the noise and run into a completely red room with some animated old guy and Chinese lanterns everywhere. Ornate fake-gold statues point toward the other door.

"She went that way!" They say.

The man by the drum gives a derisive laugh. "She's pathetic," he says as he beats the drum with one mallet.

I yell, "Fuck off, dude," as I sprint out the door. It feels good. It feels good to yell. Way better than feeling sorry for myself.

I keep going and run into another blue room. I hear voices chattering above. There are saints all around the ceiling. One says in a bored voice, "If you're looking for the whore, she went that way." The saint doesn't even bother to point, just vaguely waves a staff around.

I say to them, "You are assholes," and I hear a lot of huffing and well-I-nevers as I run through the room.

The tiger roars again from somewhere, but I hear something else through all the music playing everywhere. I hear grunts and glass crunching. And I hear two girl voices yelling out.

Violet says, "Ash, grab this," and then I hear a huge thwunk.

I round the corner onto a cobblestone street and stop to look at the scene in front of me.

There's a jester quietly repeating the word "freak," lying

on the ground, and turning in a circle. Part of his head is dented in.

Ashley stands with a wooden leg in her hands, breathing hard. Violet is against the wall, breathing hard, too, blood trailing down her neck again.

And then Dylan comes into my view and stomps on the jester's face. The thing stops saying "freak" and lies still.

Dylan's face is contorted in anger, a look I've never seen before. Dylan is chill—nothing bothers him. But this Dylan is standing tall, breathing hard, and looking down at the thing with contempt.

"Freak my dick, motherfucker," he says through huge breaths. Then he looks up at me and his eyes melt.

I feel my eyes melt, too. It's Dylan. It's *my* Dylan. John, Dylan, whatever . . .

I give him a small smile. I know it's a sad smile, but it's a smile.

And I know this deep inside. He is always my Dylan, my family. He is always Dylan to me. He is always in my life, no matter what form that takes.

I walk over to the group, careful to step over the broken jester on the ground. There is silence for a second as we stare around at each other.

Finally, my lip twitches into a smile. I say to Ashley, "So you're a leg woman, huh?"

"Wha?" she says, then remembers the wooden leg she has in her hands. She drops it and snorts in an awkward way. Then she smiles at me, but, like, a smile of "are we cool?" and, "what do you think?" and "holy shit, right?"

Then, from the other room, we hear Paul scream.

PAUL

One tiger is bad. Two tigers . . . well. I see my short life pass before my eyes. Violet is there, at the end. Beautiful, sweet, taken-advantage-of—did I mention beautiful?—Violet.

One of the tigers lunges forward and grabs my arm in his teeth, making me scream, pushing pain into my peripheral vision in a way I've never experienced before. I grab a violin and smash the tiger in the head, and the tiger lets go. But now it's me and two tigers in a standoff. And all I have is a broken violin, the curvy part swinging by the strings. What I wouldn't give for a sword now, Captain Tidbittles.

The tigers are below a sign that says TOUR THIS WAY with an arrow pointing down, like it's pointing to the tigers. *Do NOT go on that tour*, I think to myself and almost giggle.

Almost. Because I slowly back up to the other end of the room by the other door, and I assess my situation. The tigers have teeth, and muscles, and claws, and hunger. I have a broken violin. And my arm hurts so bad I can barely raise it.

Not great. Tour terminated.

One of the tigers growls and takes a step toward me, but then I feel a whoosh of air on all sides of me and someone physically bumps into me from behind, hurting my arm.

"Oh, sorry," I hear. Violet.

It's Violet.

Violet! My body sings.

"Fuck-a-doodle-doo," says Dylan.

And then Ashley says, "Of course it's a tiger. Because what else would it be?"

Gretchen says, "Where are those dolls when you need them?"

Every part of me is smiling. They're here. They're here. My friends, my Violet. They're here.

But my smile disappears fast. There is still the small matter of the two tigers in front of us. That probably now think they just hit the lottery in people meat.

The tigers growl again. And something hurtles past my head.

It's a wooden leg. You know. A wooden leg. Because what else would go flying through the air here? The tigers jump and move back.

Ashley says, "Yes, Violet!" And then I can feel people move and come back and I see objects being hurled in front of me. I'm too afraid to take my eyes off the beasts, so I watch as a milk jug, a staff, canning equipment, bottles, and even what looks like a pipe fly at them. With each object the tigers growl a little more but keep moving back. But they still haven't given up, and I know pretty soon they'll get that we don't really have anything to keep them away from us. And then it's not just me in trouble. It's everyone.

So I do something crazy.

Taking the violin, I sprint full tilt at them and scream in my loudest voice possible. The scream comes from deep inside my gut, from some memory of some pain, of some threat. It comes from my dad dying and from not knowing how to act and from being responsible when I was just a kid and being scared all the time and my life sucking and school and sports and LARPing and friends and girlfriends and Rhinehart and world hunger and racism and sexism and all isms everywhere and child soldiers and the Holocaust and the pure fucking unadulterated scariness of life.

I scream.

And then I stop one second before I reach them, because they haven't moved.

Well. Shit.

They have stopped growling at me. They have stopped growling and they are looking up at me, panting. And then, like they're bored, they turn around and walk away, out the door, into the rest of the House. I peek around the corner at them. A tail twitches out of sight, and then I pop back into the room, feeling like I'm going to pass out.

It's quiet for a second, like awkward quiet, and I can't think of anything to say. Sort of embarrassing to give it all you've got and bore some tigers.

Dylan pats my shoulder. "Dude, that scared the shit out of me, anyway."

Not the best compliment, but I'll take it anyway.

DYLAN

So, coolest dude in school's got issues.

But don't we all, yo? I pat him on the shoulder like guys do.

Everyone laughs at my joke and I feel warmth spread through me. But then I hear the jester's voice saying "freak" in my ear and cold creeps in.

No one's talking about what happened in that café. No one's talking period. We're barely even looking at each other. I know they're thinking about what a phony baloney I am. I know they all think I'm two-faced, that I'm some weirdo religious dude. But really, I didn't want to let anyone down, that's all. I didn't want to hurt anybody's feelings.

Gretch says, "So, what's next? Think hard. How many rooms?" She looks at me and says, "Do you remember?" I can see she's trying hard not to be judgy. But I hurt her, and my Gretch isn't the most forgiving horse on this merry-go-round.

I clear my throat, but Violet jumps in. Girl can see I'm uncomfortable, I'm pretty sure. Love the Violet.

She says, "We have the carousel room next, I think. Then there's this big mechanical room—maybe called the 'cask room'?—then a café, doll carousels . . ." Her shoulders slump and we all groan. She says, "I think we even pass those twice. Shoot."

Gretchen swallows, then says, "And then what?"

Ashley jumps in, "I'm pretty sure there are a bunch of doll-houses and then a huge circus-like room. That one's going to

be a bitch. And then I can't remember what comes after that."
Violet's face is blank, too.

I gather my courage like a bunch of fucking flowers on a hill-side. Gretch knows I've been here so I might as well help, yo. I remember the next displays because I thought they were so cool. "I'm pretty sure after that we pass some rooms with knights in them, like, playing out a scene. Behind glass, duders," I say, as I see everybody's faces go white. "But we'll have to go through fast because, you know, knights and shit." I stop and think. "And then . . ."

And then I remember. "And then the doll carousels again, but this time up close and personal. And I think there are, like," I practically whisper the next part because I don't even want to think about it myself, "the four horsemen of the apocalypse up there." I clear my throat.

No one talks. I don't know how we'll make it through any of it, let alone the apocalypse mofos. Especially with that info-dump in the café hanging over us like a GD bomb waiting to go off.

Ashley says after a minute, "SO! To recap: We have, like, five more rooms to go through, each with their own psychotic OR nice inhabitants, we're never sure which. We have two tigers roaming ahead of us. And anything in the rooms we've gone through before can come and follow us. Maybe even an OCEAN that we could, like, drown in. And then, to get outside—if that asshole demon guy will even let us, which, let me tell you, sounds pretty fucking unlikely—we have to go through a sea of dolls AND the four horsemen of the apocalypse?"

Again, no one talks.

Finally Gretchen says, "Well. We better get going."

GRETCHEN

Maybe 20 minutes have passed since I was in that blue room, thinking I would just let the House kill me. But now I feel something else, something strong, muster in me. Maybe it's because I found everyone again, even if they all hate me. At least I don't want to die now.

But I still can't look anyone in the eye. I can barely look at Dylan. I can't look at Ashley. And Violet and Paul . . . well, shit.

I don't see this having a happy ending.

But whatever, we're here now. "Okay, so we have the carousel room next, right? Let's just do one room at a time. One thing at a time."

Paul nods. "Yeah, good plan. But, you should know, two mini-centaurs told me there's a fight going on in there between the angels and . . . well, I don't know what else. Other mini-centaurs maybe?"

I don't even blink. Any other day, Paul would be committed to an inpatient mental ward for that sentence.

Violet brightens up. I see this from the corner of my eye since I can't seem to look anyone directly in the face. I'm pretty sure I have an EBT sign hanging over my head. TAKER.

She says, "If they're fighting, maybe that's good. They'll leave us alone."

Paul looks at her sort of sideways and nods. "Yeah, that's smart. Let's just try to stay out of the way, not get noticed."

A thump sounds from another room behind us. I say, "We should go. Now. Who knows what's coming?"

Ashley says under her breath, "In so many ways."

ASHLEY

Gretchen smiled at me. She smiled at me. It's not making out, but it's something.

We start walking, Paul leading the way with his tiger-bitten arm tucked in, like he's holding a book in his armpit or something. Violet's looking at his arm and she puts her hand out as if to touch it, but then pulls her hand back. Paul doesn't even notice. His temple is throbbing and he has this look on his face like he's about ready to kill something.

I'm glad we're all together and all, but I'm way more glad he's in front.

We walk. Paul, then Violet to his right, one step behind. Me, then Gretchen one step behind on my right. Dylan one step behind on her left. We're staggered, like some weird-ass croquet set.

Fractured.

We come to a door with a long ramp up to a small landing. Paul turns and starts up the ramp without saying a word, and we follow. As we near a turn, I can hear a loud male voice say, "Fight, you creatures, fight! Damn ye!"

I do not want to go into this fucking room.

Paul turns to us. "I think we should hold hands. We'll look for the door and move straight to it. Yes?" When did he get all decide-y? Regardless, we all nod. I nod so hard my teeth chatter. I flex my sore-ass feet in my towel bundles.

Gretchen says, "Where is the door . . . anyone remember?"

I remember and swear under my breath. "It's through a monster's mouth. The doorway, I think, is to the left, but it's a monster's mouth." I close my eyes and say again, "Fuck."

I feel a collective sigh ripple through the group.

Gretchen says, "Well, let's hope that mouth doesn't bite down when we go through it, I guess."

I swallow. Really? This is my life? Hoping I don't get digested by a monster? I am totally suing this place when I get out. After I disown my parents.

A hand takes mine—a soft one—and then another soft one but definitely male. On my right, Gretchen holds my hand. On my left, Dylan holds my hand.

Okayyyyyy. Awkward.

I look at Dylan from the corner of my eye and he is bouncing a leg and looking to his left. Gretchen, when I scope her out on the other side, is looking to the right. I clear my throat.

Paul says, "Let's go," and Gretchen's hand tightens on mine. Reflex? God, I hope not. I hope it means she doesn't hate me. Or, maybe even something more. Hope leaks out of me—of course she hates me. I have been nothing but an asshole to her.

Weirder still? Dylan squeezes my hand, too. The guy may be a liar, but I have to give him this: he's got some major kindness in him. For all intents and purposes, he should be mad as shit at me. I squeeze his hand back.

We walk up the ramp like some line of preschool kids and stop in the doorway, all of us looking around the corner but hiding our bodies.

Shit's gotten real. Music has started up—more manic calliope music—and in front of us is the biggest, weirdest carousel I've ever seen, starting to spin slowly. Populated with Mermaids, knights, tigers, unicorns, and pretty much any mythical creature I've ever read about. As it turns, faster and faster, different creatures wrench themselves off. There's a scraping of metal on metal as they take themselves—poles and all—*off the carousel.*

But creepier still? They're getting off the carousel to join others on the ground, some with poles, some not, to fight the swooping mannequins with wings that have begun attacking them.

Swooping. Mannequins. With. Wings.

Angels, House style. Awesome.

In the middle of the fairy-tale wet dream of creatures on the floor, a tiny centaur in an old-fashioned British military jacket glances over at Paul. "Young sir! I see you came. Help us fight these monstrous angels!" He stops and grunts as a mannequin whose wig is falling off swoops down and grabs him by the hair. His four legs scramble in the air.

Another little centaur, this one who looks like a total whore from olden times, grabs onto one of his hoofs and the angel drops him. When the military guy drops, the she-centaur says, "Git yer dirty hands off 'im!"

And the military guy says, "Millie, you saved me yet again."

The mannequin-angel lets out a banshee-like scream and swoops away after another target. I see her land on a pole that runs through a unicorn who has wrenched himself free from the carousel. The angel perches on the pole like a bat and grabs the unicorn's horn, wrenching his head back and forth. Then she leans down and bites the unicorn right in the neck. Blood spurts everywhere.

"Holy shitballs," I say, and can hear the panic in my wavery voice.

Banshee screams echo around the room and in the middle of it, giggles.

Another angel swoops down and picks up a squealing pig that has wrenched itself off the carousel, and bites into it, tearing off its skin. Blood drips down her chin and the flopping pig in front of her stops flopping. The angel giggles, flesh still in her teeth. Then she takes off into the air again.

Violet flips around and pulls Paul with her. She says, voice shaking. "I emphatically don't want to go in this room."

VIOLET

There is blood everywhere. And Paul won't look at me, though he's holding my hand. No one will, really. No one is really looking at anyone else. We're together but still alone.

There is blood everywhere and there are angels swooping down and biting through pigs and we have to run through a monster's mouth.

I think I can safely say this is a low point in my young life. I think I can safely say I'm going to die in here.

The screams are getting worse. Paul's hand squeezes mine. I hope against hope that this is deliberate and not just a reaction to the scene out there. I don't want to die knowing he hates me.

The carouselers are getting massacred. I see another angel swoop down and grab a rabbit ridden by a tiny knight. The knight grabs his sword and plunges it into the angel's side. The angel drops the rabbit but grabs the rider by the head as the rabbit drops. And yanks the rider's head off. The sword clatters to the floor. Blood splatters everywhere. Blood blood blood.

I say, feeling bile rise in my throat, "Aren't they supposed to be inanimate? How do they have blood?"

Paul suddenly turns around to us. "Listen. I have to help them. I have to help. I have to . . . The angels are killing them. You guys stay here." Then he finally looks at me and gives a weird little shrug. "Plus. You know. I know how to use a sword."

"Wait!" I yell and try to hold onto his hand to stop him, but his fingers slip out of mine before I can react and he runs full-tilt into the melee. Angels swoop down at him and he falls on his knees on the floor and uses the blood to slide several feet to the sword, like an insanely macabre superhero Slip'N Slide.

Holy schmolies, that was way cool and really gross. Plus: sword. A real one.

He picks up the sword and starts slashing at angels, his other arm tucked into his body.

Behind me, Ashley screams, "PAUL! WHAT THE HELL?"

I turn around, not knowing what words to use to explain what I'm going to do next. To explain that Paul will not be in there alone.

I give the rest of them a "sorry" look and shrug. Then I swallow and run full on into the bloodbath.

Gretchen yells, "Violet!" But her voice disappears in the screams around me.

I find another sword—this one shorter and blunted—on the ground. It will have to do. I duck as an angel tries to grab my head, and I feel my hair fly as the swoosh of air hits me. I jump over bodies and slip on the blood. Something knocks me in the head—right on my bad ear—and I fall over for just a second, but find my feet again. I run over to Paul, who is breathing heavily. His eyes go wide when he sees me.

"Go back!" He yells to me and then takes a swing at an angel swooping by. He hits it right in the face and the thing screams and swoops away. An angel comes at him from behind, so I push him away and swing my sword at it. I catch it in the arm and it swoops away.

I look at Paul and yell, "No!" I stare hard at him. Something in his face softens and his eyes search mine. He's about to say something, but he's pushed aside by a huge St. Bernard just as an angel comes at him from above. I duck, too, putting my hands in the softness of the St. Bernard. The dog says, "Watch your back!" then makes a running leap into a mound of angels that are tearing apart a mermaid on the floor. He picks up an angel in his teeth and shakes it hard, throwing it into a cart at the side of the carousel.

In my peripheral vision, I see angels dropping from the sky left and right. And then feel bodies standing next to mine.

"Jesus Christ, why are we getting involved?" Ashley stands beside me, wielding a long bloody spear. Gretchen is on the other side of her, swinging a metal pipe with bits of hair stuck to it. Dylan has inexplicably found a torch that he is swinging around like a baseball bat.

This, it seems, is what we do now. Stand in front of mortal danger. Alone together.

The five of us back up into each other so that we can see on every side. Paul says, almost apologetically, "I couldn't just stand there."

Nobody says anything, but I can hear each of us breathing, I can tell who's who by the cadence of their inhalations, the sound of their panting.

The fighting has lessened, a swoop here and there, and the little captain centaur, his face a bloody mess, his scalp showing oozy patches where his hair has been torn out, gallops up to us and speaks to Paul. "Young sir, you've fought bravely. We can hold off these angels—it is a fair fight now. But you, you must get through. Go now. The mouth is closing."

And sure enough, the monster mouth that we need to go through to get out is opening and closing. The teeth go up and down—chomp, chomp. I can imagine my leg snapping in there. I swallow. A low growl rumbles through the doorway, audible even over the groans of the fallen carouselers and angels.

I take a quick look around. The place looks like a horror movie. Blood, body parts, and hair coat the floor. All of us are covered and smeared with blood. And our choice? Stay here, or go through the monster's mouth.

Dylan says, "Dudes. Let's go be monster poop."

DYLAN

Gretch says, "We have to time this right. Who goes first?"

Ashley sticks her spear up at an angel flying by, but misses. She says, "You go first. We'll go in the order we're standing."

Meaning Ashley goes last. Crazy. I thought she'd be more likely to use our bodies as monster entree, not let us go first.

A pang of guilt kicks at me. Not nice, bro, thinking things like that. So I say, "I'll go last," and then pull Ashley in front of me. Gretch flips her head around to me, but I yell, "You need to go now."

Because, sure enough, the mouth is open. And fucker's going to close in a second if I've got the rhythm right. Gretchen is the closest and she has to go right now or wait and keep us all waiting in this brutal nightmare of a room.

You know, in Vacation Bible School, they never told us that angels were douchemunches. They didn't tell us much, though, except: you'll burn in hell for masturbating, gay people are the devil, and liberals are godless, soul-sucking, country-hating, baby-killing communists who will be left when we rapture. I never really believed any of it, though. I don't know much, but in the Bible shit I've read it seems that Jesus was a way cool dude who probably would have hated VBS and would have DEF given all his money to the poor. Unlike my parents and the people in my church. But *I'm* the liar here, supposedly.

I nod at Gretch and she says, "Make it through. All of you." And then she grits her teeth and flips her head around.

She runs the two steps to the mouth. I hold my breath.

Just before she jumps through, she slips on some blood, messing up her torque. She tries to regain her balance, but yo, she is half-in and half-out of the mouth. The mouth about to chomp.

"GRETCHEN!" I yell and a panic flame shoots through my body. Just as the monster's teeth crunch down, Gretch tucks herself into a ball and somersaults in. Teeth slam down and she's out of sight.

I hold my chest and sag against Ashley in front of me. Fuck-a-doodle-doo. An angel swoops down at us, but all I do is stick my torch straight up in the air—thank you St. Bernard, dude dog, with your actually useful basket of first aid, including a lighter—and burn the fucker. It screams and swoops off.

The monster opens its mouth again.

Violet yells, "Go, Paul!" But instead, he pushes her forward and she has no choice but to run for it or wait for the next run.

The mouth, I can tell, is going up and down faster, so Violet speeds up and dives in, just as the mouth closes.

Two in.

The mouth is def moving faster now, so Ashley says, "We need to get closer and just dive in, when we can," and both Paul and me nod.

Fuck. The mouth is a chomping machine. The air from the movement is like a fan blowing in my face. Up, down, up, down . . . Maybe 4 seconds between chomps now.

We move to the side of the mouth and fight off any angels that come at us almost like we're so bored of it. Fucking angels. I almost wish for the dolls to come back. At least they can't fly.

After a few chomps, Paul yells, "Jump, Ashley!" She's taking in the chomping of the mouth, silently counting—I can see her lips move. Like girl's doing double Dutch or something. She takes a look at us and then takes a deep breath.

Then she dives. A tooth chomps on a piece of her foot

bandage that has unraveled, but she's through. The teeth now have a bloody bandage attached to them. I stifle a totally inappropriate laugh-dagger that shoots through me. Monster dude has some Ashley between his teeth.

I look to Paul and am about to say, "You go, man," when the guy yells, "Don't wait for me." And then he shoves me hard.

I see teeth in front of me and then dark space. I land in something sticky and wet and feel hands pulling me up.

Violet's eyes are the first I can see, almost glowing in the dark. "Where's Paul?" She says, voice panic-shaky. And then the ground below me moves.

PAUL

The teeth are chomping so fast now, I don't think I can get through.

I put my arm out to test it, but my arm almost gets chomped off.

I'm stuck in here with deranged angels. Deranged angels I've pissed off.

Oops.

Violet is on the other side of the teeth. And I have been avoiding her looks this whole time like a big jerk. Now she'll never know. She'll never know how I feel. And I'll never get to kiss her.

An angel swoops by my head and smacks my face with something sharp. I feel blood run down my cheek and then look up to see the angel fall like a dead lump of flesh, an arrow sticking out of her heart. Captain Tidbittles runs to me. "We'll help."

Before I can react, a unicorn with a pole through it and a huge bite on its neck trots up to us. Just as another angel swoops at me, something jumps at it and grabs it in its teeth.

A saber-toothed tiger.

Whaa?

I feel something furry and muscly rub against me, sleek. I feel a rumbling that moves through me; it's so deep.

The other tiger is rubbing up against me. And purring. It knocks its head under my hand for a pet. So. I pet it.

I am petting a saber-toothed tiger.

It licks my hand. I decide to just run with it. "What's the plan?"

The captain says, "Indeed. Sparkles here will stick his pole between the beast's jaws and keep them open long enough for you to pass through."

I can't help myself. Some things you have to take a stand on. "Sparkles? Really? The unicorn's name is Sparkles? Also, we just met a really jerky unicorn . . ."

The unicorn gives me an indignant look and whinnies. The captain looks genuinely confused. "What's wrong with the name Sparkles? And I'll have you know this unicorn is of great character!"

The tiger puts its head under my hand again. I pet it, feeling more than a little uneasy. Nice kitty. Blood drips down my cheek and I swipe at it.

Okay. Sparkles. The unicorn of integrity. I hope that's true. "Won't the mouth chomp down on, uh, Sparkles?" I cringe a little. I have dressed in tights and a cape, quoted Shakespeare to myself constantly, and danced a medieval dance with my mother, yet saying the unicorn's name makes my whole body cringe. I mean, come on. Sparkles.

The captain pets the unicorn and the unicorn whinnies again and looks back at the captain. He hesitates. "It's a possibility." But I can tell by both their expressions that it's more than a possibility.

"Why are you helping me?" I ask.

The captain winks. "I can't just stand here and watch, can I? You didn't, young sir. You were brave." He leans into me, and I lean down to look him in the eye. They are bright blue and intense. "Make this worth it. Do not let Sparkles' sacrifice be in vain."

I wait a second before answering. I'm not sure it's right to let this creature sacrifice itself for me. But then I see its proud, fierce eyes and the blood running down its neck.

If I were him, I'd want to die fast in a monster's teeth rather than slow from an angel's bite.

I nod and feel my eyes fill up. "Thank you," is all I can say.

"You are the best unicorn I have ever met." And it's true. Sparkles stomps a hoof.

We turn to the monster's teeth, which are now chomping down at an alarming rate.

The captain says, "Okay. We must time this right. Here we go, Sparkles."

"One . . ."

"Two . . ." I see the unicorn's muscles bunch up.

"Three!"

The unicorn jumps and somehow manages to lodge itself in the monster's mouth at the very part where it could stop the chomping. There is a 12-inch gap for me to jump through. Already I see the pole in the unicorn bending.

"NOW!" yells the captain.

I jump.

I land on a pile of people and hear a pop and a whinny. I flip around, thinking Sparkles has been crushed. But there is no blood on the teeth.

Sparkles made it. SPARKLES MADE IT!

I whoop loud and yell, "YES, SPARKLES!"

Somehow, I am lifted up and put on my feet. The floor moves and the walls are red and squishy. Something wet and gooey drips down my front, my head.

Oh, god. We're in an esophagus. The monster's esophagus.

Ashley says to the rest of the group, "Ew! Monster spit. And P.S. I think Paul's got head trauma. He just yelled 'yes Sparkles.'"

Blood and monster spit drip down my chin. But Sparkles the unicorn made it. And for the first time in a long time, I don't feel scared.

ASHLEY

"Sparkles is a unicorn," Paul says as we try to make our way through the grossest hallway ever. "A really brave unicorn." Walking in this throat makes me feel bad for every single hamburger I've eaten. But at least it's squishy and isn't so hard on my untoweled foot.

The hallway is totally dark now because the mouth has stopped moving and is closed shut. How we all made it, I'll never know.

But clearly there's some brain damage among us. I let it go, though. "Okay. Yay, Sparkles the unicorn. Anyway, what's next?" The pain in my foot is intensifying.

Violet, who is leading the way, reaches the end of the esophagus and steps out. I hear her feet squish.

She turns back and says, "Cask room."

We all join her on the carpet, out of the godforsaken monster throat. I am officially never going to be a surgeon.

The room is huge. I mean, like, huge. It's cavernous, but of course, like the rest of this stupid hoarder House, it's packed with stuff. The room is lit by red lanterns everywhere, so the whole place has a dim red pall.

The things I can see are gigantic. Big casks with asshole smiling male masks on the front of them. Bridges that crisscross the room in different places. A cannon. The largest organ I've ever seen. Freud much, House? Figurines of saints and woodland creatures. Fake trees.

And then I hear the dreaded patter of little feet.

Gretchen says, "Oh, fuck me."

I clear my throat.

We see a doll on a bridge in the middle of the room. It keeps running, though.

Violet sighs.

Paul says, "How'd they get in here? The monster mouth is clearly closed."

Dylan adds, "They must have run ahead. I mean . . . from the beginning of the tour. You know what I'm saying?"

Violet looks around, brow furrowed. She steps up to a cask with a face on it. The face is a weathered green, like copper left in the rain.

"Can you help us?" she asks.

Can't say I blame her for trying—nothing makes sense in this place—but I still say: "Jesus, Violet. Give it up. This place wants us dead."

"No," Paul says. "Not all of it, remember? Some things are fine. Like Sparkles."

Before I can say, "duh, I know," and "what's with you and that unicorn?" the cask says, "The young man speaks the truth. But I've got to be honest with you. I'm afraid I *do* want you dead."

It actually sounds remorseful. Whatever.

"We need to get through this room, *now*," I growl. I start limping forward. As I pass a small statue of a wizard guy with a long beard and a staff, it says, "I can help."

Violet hears it, too, and catches up with me.

She says, "Thank you!"

I glare at her. When will she learn not to trust these things? Or anyone for that matter? She is way too nice. This world will eat her alive. This House will, literally.

Violet asks, "Do you know how this works? Like, were you able to talk until we came into the world?"

The wizard stretches himself out and yawns. He's only about knee-height, but I step back anyway.

"Oh, no. This is why I'm more than happy to help. I've been

stuck in this position for ages, you see, until you came in. I've played this game before. But sadly, I lost. I'll help you win, though! At least I'll try! The only thing we can do really is try." He smiles big.

Violet says, "Aha!"

I stare at her. We all do.

She says, like she's explaining to her goddamn kindergarten class. "I suspected as much from the last room. Remember when we stood on the ramp to the carousel and only heard one voice talking? And then we got to the room and this huge war started? I think we 'activate' a room or something when we enter it."

The wizard says cheerfully, "Oh, and after that, we all can follow you, as luck would have it. We don't go back to sleep once you're gone. You've set us in motion."

I nod. "So, like in the whale room, that's why we didn't drown right away. Because the room was only activated once we were in there."

Violet nods, her eyes shining.

Dylan says. "Sweet! So how does that help?"

We look at each other.

Violet says, "I suppose it really doesn't."

But I interrupt because all of a sudden I am furious with this whole thing. Everything. The House, my feet, Gretchen, everything. "It doesn't help. Except now we KNOW we can't get out of this House. Because everything is alive and it's a DEATH TRAP."

Tears come to my eyes, but I refuse to let them fall. "Let's just go. Let's just get this over with." I charge ahead, limping hard, tears finally breaking through and falling.

I can hear them walking behind me.

The wizard, from way behind says, "Oh, I'll come with you and help. Don't fear!"

Great. A stalking wizard.

The room is so big that only when I go over the first bridge do I finally get a sense of where the exit is. There is one long hallway. One way out looks to be by the organ. The other way takes us down a winding hall that leads to somewhere I can't see.

I remember this now. The way by the organ leads to a café.

With huge windows . . .

I turn around fast, almost knocking Gretchen over. I didn't realize she was so close. Sweat starts in my armpits. Swallowing, I say, "There's another café over there. It's got these huge windows. Maybe we can get out."

There's laughter all around, but I don't even bother looking at the animal heads or figures or statues or whatever it's coming from.

The wizard says, "Maybe!" And peeks around Paul, who is bringing up the rear of our group, with a smile.

Jesus Christ, that is one perky wizard.

Gretchen says softly, "It's worth a try." Her breath is close to me. Out of the corner of my eye, I see a suit of armor. And I notice that some of the figurines look like they've moved closer.

I keep my voice low and say, "This is a good time to sprint through the room again. We are going to that door." I point to where the organ is and then trace my finger around the path. "After this bridge, we have a pathway, then another bridge, and then the door. On my count, we'll go fast and try to outrun anything that might come after us."

The wizard stage whispers, "Okay," and gives us a thumbs up.

All five of us look back at him. I shake my head. Gretchen says, "Jesus."

And then I count, "One. Two. Three," and sprint.

GRETCHEN

Ashley runs faster than I think she possibly could with one of her feet detoweled. Must be from all her personal trainers and swanky gym memberships. Still, somewhere in my brain I am admiring her calf muscles and, well, if I'm honest, other parts. This isn't the first time I've checked out a girl—but it is totally the first time I've checked out a girl I hate. Or used to hate. Or something. I don't know anything anymore.

I remember Dylan and look back. He's doing okay. The wizard, however, is totally huffing.

He says between pants, "You guys . . . fast . . . wait . . ." But I roll my eyes. Losing this little guy wouldn't totally suck. Though he does seem harmless.

But so did my dad. So did Dylan.

Anger shoots through me and my legs are running faster. Running past statues that have begun to throw things at us. A tree branch flies at me from nowhere. A metal drinking cup. A tiara. Something I don't see smacks me in the head and bounces off. Hoots and hollers echo through the room and a crow caws from somewhere up above.

"Run, humans, run. Run, humans, run," I hear, and then it becomes a chant. A super creepy, dickish chant.

Every once in a while, I see doll faces peek out from behind things. But so far, nothing is actually chasing us. Progress.

We reach the door. Above it is another ram head and a deer head. The ram head says, "Oh, THOSE humans. I thought we'd gotten rid of those. Isn't this game over already? Have some manners and just die."

And then we're through the door and running down a hall to the main café that is surprisingly modern looking, with white tables and chairs on a black and white floor, and a huge white sculpture in the middle of the room.

And wall-sized windows. Everywhere.

Windows that look to the outside.

Where our classmates are, standing on a ramp.

They are milling about and talking to each other and texting on their phones. They are right there, on the other side of the windows. Right there.

Without stopping, we all run to the windows and start pounding on them.

"Help, you motherfuckers!" Ashley screams, banging on the glass. Dylan throws his body against the glass, leaving grease and blood smudges; his arm has started bleeding again and I notice his face is super cut up. Violet pounds with her fists and then scratches at the windows, saying, "Please! Please, help us!" Paul uses flat palms to smack the window and yells a staccato, "Hey. Hey you. You!"

No one looks at us. Not one person. They should be able to hear us but they clearly can't.

We are on the inside looking out. And no one can see us.

Violet turns around and slides down the glass, crying openly. Paul walks over to her and sits next to her, but doesn't touch her. His arm has stopped bleeding and he can use it, I know. He just doesn't.

Dylan stops throwing himself at the window and sits down at a table across from the windows. Ashley turns around, her face white and stricken, and sits down at a different table. I don't say a word but just stare out the window for another second. Then I take a chair and put it between the two tables and sit down.

We hear panting, and the wizard comes into view: "Man, you guys run fast. Oh look! More humans!" He points outside, face lighting up with a smile. We all look at him and his face falls. "Okay. I'll just . . . I'll just let you have a minute or so," and then he wanders off to the kitchen area of the café, the clicking of his staff on the tile the only sound besides our heavy breathing.

I put my face in my hands. No one speaks for a full five minutes.

After an eternity, Ashley clears her throat.

She says, "Listen. It's pretty clear we're all going to die in here. So. I just wanted to say I'm, you know. I'm super, um . . . I'm sorry."

I look up at her. Tears are in her eyes and she says to me, "Gretchen, I know I have been horrible to you. Horrible. But, it's because I've been jealous of you, that's all. I've been jealous that you don't give a shit what anyone else thinks and you wear awesome clothes, which I would never admit to anyone. And because . . ." She looks up and then down at her hands. "And because I *have* had a crush on you for a long time."

I don't know what to say. The words hit me in the chest, slide down into my stomach, and turn into butterflies.

And then the butterflies turn into angry caterpillars.

"Ashley, what are you talking about? You hate me. And now that you know . . . my thing . . . I'm sure it's only worse." I can't look at her, but I feel tears in my eyes, too. The words "trailer trash" repeat themselves over and over and over again in my head.

After a few seconds, she says, "I'm trying to apologize here. And I don't give a crap if you're on food stamps."

I wince. "Bullshit, you don't care. That's ALL you care about. You and your friends with your name brand shit and your complete and utter dedication to being assholes to people. That demon guy said it—you think I'm a mooch. You think my mom who can barely stand up but works twelve-hour shifts and STILL can't afford to put food on the table is a mooch. Well, fuck you." Now I look at her, wishing I could actually kill her with my eyes.

"That's not fair," she says. She's shaking. "I didn't know your situation. And anyway, I don't see YOU trying to talk to me at school. I don't see you trying."

I can't help it, I snort loud. "Why in all that is holy would I want to talk to you? You wouldn't give me the time of day!"

Ashley stands up, too, the tears gone now. "Oh, please. As if you don't know this is how the world works. Can you blame me for being what I'm supposed to be? Do you think I have a *choice*? If you were in my situation, you're telling me you'd act differently. No fucking way. You'd be wearing Prada like a champ."

Anger is full-on raging in me now. "Of course you have a choice! I would NEVER be like you. If it were me, I would grow some fucking courage and actually, oh, I don't know, come out? Maybe talk to other people at school?"

Ashley hobbles closer to me, "As if! What is this the fucking *Breakfast Club* now? I didn't make these rules! And me, coming out? That's laughable. My family has made an empire on family values. Do you know what that means? *I'd ruin my family, Gretchen.* Try living with that. This world is harsh and I'm a goddamn realist—I am *surviving*. And you survive the best way you know how, too."

Paul's voice rings out from by the window, quiet. "No. *The Breakfast Club* is for white people." His brown eyes are hard. "I don't think either of you get to talk about how hard you have it. Try being the only black guy in Aryan Fucking Nation, Wisconsin. Or, you know, anywhere in this country."

Ashley rolls her eyes and sits down again, "Oh, please. People worship you. Everybody at school thinks you're cool—you don't even have to try. *Because* you are black."

Paul stands up, shaking. He raises his voice louder than I've ever heard him. "Yeah, they *worship* me. Because what white person *doesn't love black people*? White people love us so much they kill us, am I right? I am a 4.0 student and have done NOTHING wrong EVER and still I'm followed around by fucking mall security cops. And real cops. Or just guys on the streets with their white daughters. And if I want to live, god fucking forbid I wear a hoodie! Or play music. Or drive a car. Or walk on the streets! There is no safe place for me, none. No safe place because of the skin I live in. But that's all right because I'm *cool*. Lucky fucking me." And then tears start streaming down his face. "You have no idea, Ashley. You never will. You and people like you . . . you can just fuck off."

I can't help it, I feel triumphant. I look at Ashley with my eyebrows up. Check and mate, you hot bitch, you.

But Paul says, "I don't know why you look so smug, Gretchen. It's not like you're any better."

I start. "Excuse me?" I flip around to Paul.

"Like you aren't a hypocrite. Ashley's right. All of us survive the best we can."

Anger shoots through me again. "Fuck you, Paul. You don't know me."

He laughs and shakes his head. "First, don't try to pretend you don't have it easy by being white, okay? Don't act like you don't get a pass because of that."

Now, I'm pissed. "Fucking duh. Yeah, it's true. I've got white privilege. I never said I didn't. And I can't help it—I didn't ask for it."

Paul laughs. "Yeah, poor you."

Ashley says, snorting, "Well, by that logic, can I help it if I have a leg up? Where's the fucking understanding for me?"

I flip around to her but then turn back around to Paul. "Tell me, Paul and Ashley, how often do you guys have to choose between paying the electric bill or the heat? How often do you cook for your mom? Huh? How often do you worry if you can eat that day? If your mom will have to go to the hospital and if she does, how you'll fucking pay for it? Ashley, when you're meeting your sex toys do you have to set it up at the library because you don't have a computer or Internet? And when you're dressing up in your little tights, Paul, are you thinking about how much they cost? What are your hard choices, you two, I want to hear.

Steak or ribs? Mercedes or Lexus?" Tears are threatening my eyes and are about to spill over.

Paul shakes his head. "You want to talk about making choices? Would you be dating John over there if you knew his parents were religious freaks?"

Dylan backs up like he's been hit. "Yo, dude. Not cool. My parents aren't freaks."

Ashley laughs a mean laugh. "Right. When is the rapture, *John Luke?*"

Dylan's face is getting beet red. "My name is Dylan, yo. But you guys, I think we should stop fighting. This isn't doing any good. We're playing right into that demon dude's hands."

Now it's my time to get mad. "Now you believe in demons, huh? Really? Really. Maybe you should talk to your pal, white Jesus—you know, the same guy who gives a shit who wins at football but thinks poor people should just starve and women should be, you know, *submissive* and shit—and pray real hard to have your name changed for real. Poor, abused guy with the two rich, hallelujah parents."

The tears start flowing freely now. Dylan takes a step closer to me and I yell, "Don't come near me!" I wipe at my eyes but start sobbing, and before I can stop myself, I get real. "I trusted you, Dylan. I trusted you! You've made a fool out of me. *For four years!*" My voice breaks at the end.

And now Dylan is crying. "Gretch, babe, I didn't want you to know. I just didn't want . . ."

He paces in the middle of the room, wiping his eyes. "I don't believe what my parents believe, okay? I mean, I'm Christian, but not that bullshit Christian that asstrolls turn into their own excuse for being dicks. That's not the life I want to lead. Like," he looks at Ashley, "I don't think gay people are going to burn in hell," looks back to me, "and I don't think, like, God made women, you know, subservient. I mean, holy fuck-grenades, Gretch, I've been dating you, right? I don't believe in most of what my church says—they have a fucking agenda, what they want you to be. My parents, yo . . . They don't know me and they don't want to. Not the real me. And I don't want to hurt their feelings so I go along, you know? I survive. And with you, I didn't want you to feel bad and hate me for where I come from. My parents and their whole worldview . . . they're just terrified. They are terrified of this world they, like, don't know anymore, you know? They hold onto this rigid way of thinking because . . . loving different people like Jesus told people to is too hard sometimes. Because love doesn't fit in neat boxes." He stops and his voice turns into a hiccup. "Like how we love each other."

I put my head in my hands and sob. I can't breathe.

He goes on, kneeling beside me. "You know the real me, Gretch. I swear. But my parents would die if they knew who I am—who I REALLY am—or what I believe. They'd fucking hate me, yo. I'm talking disowned. You have it hard, Gretch, but your mom loves you just the way you are. I would love that. Try to understand, baby. I wanted to be loved by you for who I am, too."

My heart breaks in two, but I can't bring myself to say anything.

Paul walks over to the window and slides down it again. "Let's face it. We're all a bunch of hypocrites. We're all pretending."

All the fight leaves me and I look up and stare out the window. He's right. Only here, in this fucked up House, are we exactly who we are.

From across the way, Violet's voice rings out. "I have something to say."

VIOLET

Dylan, Gretchen, and Ashley turn to look at me, almost like they forgot I was here. Paul turns his face toward mine—I can feel his gaze like it's a physical touch. Now that all the attention is on me, I have a hard time starting. Blood crawls to my face. My ear throbs. My hands hurt. A scrape on my side starts stinging. And that's just the physical hurt. The emotional pain is way worse.

"I want to say, that I'm sorry. For . . ." But I'm not sure what I'm sorry for. For being an idiot?

"I'm sorry because I guess I'm the biggest liar of all. Because I kept what I did with . . . Mr. Rhinehart . . . a secret. I'm sorry for being such an idiot and for doing something so gross." I put my head down. A wave of shame crashes on me so hard I am pulled under and for a minute I can't get air in my lungs. I want to disappear. I wish I'd never brought it up. Especially because no one says anything.

And then Gretchen's voice breaks through, loud and angry. She is definitely not crying now. "Why in the holy hell are YOU sorry? That asshole is a predator. That son of a bitch is a sex offender!"

Her words are like smelling salts. I snap my head up. "Oh, no. No, that's not it. I agreed to it. I mean, we waited until I was eighteen to, um . . . you know." I feel Paul shift next to me and I'm hoping against hope that a doll comes and kills me right then and there.

But then, after a beat, Ashley says, "So let me get this straight.

That disgusting dickmunch hit on you when you were seven-teen, but KNEW he shouldn't be doing that, and so he waited until your eighteenth birthday so you couldn't press charges?"

I wrinkle my eyebrows. I'd never thought of it that way. I say, "Kind of? Well, yeah. Yes. But, I mean, I agreed to it."

Dylan jumps in. His eyes are red from crying but otherwise he actually looks mad, too. "But, dudette. That asstroll is a teacher. A teacher. A really fucking bad one, too, yo, but whatevs. Anyway, he totally sought you out and preyed on you. This is some *Date-line* shit right here."

Confusion swamps over me. It appears that this group of people that two seconds ago could barely stand in the same room together feel the exact same way about this. But no. I shake my head. "No. I have to take responsibility for this. I had an affair with him. I said yes. I never stopped it."

I lean my head back against the window and let the tears stream down. I am a disgusting human being. I feel someone sit down next to me. It's Ashley.

"Girl. Look. I'm totally confused about a lot of things right now. Clearly. But I know this: there's a power dynamic here, you see? There's this thing that happens when some dickmunch in a power position uses that to get some. Do you understand? Asshole used his stupid teacher position over you. That's, like, totally predator shit, like Dylan said."

I let that soak in for a minute. Then I whisper, "But I liked the attention. I did. I liked that he chose me."

Gretchen says softly, "Of course you did. That's normal. But he chose you because he knew that he could manipulate you. Because you're nice. I'm not saying you aren't gorgeous, but . . . people like him. They do this on purpose. They pick people they know won't say no. And he's crazy manipulative because he waited until you were eighteen to do the deed. That's hella shitty in about eight different ways. This is not your fault."

Dylan bends down and takes my hand. I can feel the kindness

radiating off of him. He says, "Seriously, yo. You've never seen *Dateline?*"

Shame flushes through me, but I look up. Ashley, Gretchen, and Dylan stare at me, all with kindness. With kindness, not disgust. I start to feel a little lighter. I start to feel . . . a little mad. I remember the ways Mr. Rhinehart would make me feel bad, how he would guilt me into being with him, make sure I didn't look at anyone else. I remember trying to break it off with him and his temper tantrum. I remember at the same time him talking to another, younger girl with that same look he did with me.

I remember. This never felt right. It never did feel like something I *wanted* to do. It felt like something I *had* to do. Because I was chosen.

But I still did it.

I swallow. "If I wasn't such a pushover, maybe this wouldn't have happened. If I had some sort of backbone. If I had just said no that first time, or told someone. If I hadn't been such a . . ." I hang my head down. "A slut." My body hiccups with another sob, totally against my permission.

A soft but dry hand holds on to mine and warms me through. Paul uses his other hand to turn my face toward him and I feel the air shift as the rest of them back up. His eyes are level and kind. Serious and believable.

"You had a bad man manipulate some of the best things about you—your sweetness and trust. He is the asshole here. Not you. NOT you. You, Violet, you—are perfect."

I can't speak. I stare back with my mouth wide open. I whisper, "You don't hate me?"

Tears come to his eyes again and he shakes his head, his eyebrows crossed in confusion. "I would never hate you, Violet. Never." And then he uses the back of his hand to wipe his eyes. "Besides," he sniffs, "you want to talk bad choices? Did you hear us talking? This is the room of bad choices. And no one manipulated me into tights and a cape."

I bark out a laugh and a snot bubble comes out again.

I will always and forever have a snot bubble form around the man of my dreams.

Everyone else laughs, too, and with that, the tension breaks in the room. Dylan says to Paul, "Dude, you were fierce with that sword! Whatever the SVA is, it gave you some mad fucking skills!" He winks at me and I know he's getting the attention off of me. And I am so so so grateful for the rest of my life to Dylan for changing the subject. Dylan/John, whatever. He is the kindest freak I've ever met.

Paul says, "SCA. And it *is* dorky. But you know what? I don't care. I do have some mad skills. And I do look pretty good in tights."

I hope to see that one day. But I look at him and say what I've been thinking this whole time, "The way you rushed in at the carousel . . . Paul, you are one of the bravest people I've ever met."

Paul smiles the happiest smile and tears come to his eyes again. I want to hug him all over and pet him and kiss the living crap out of him. We look into each other's eyes, and he leans in just slightly, moving his eyes toward my lips. I lean in, too, my whole body screaming and mind going crazy it'shappeningit's happeningit'shappening, and then, Dylan says, "Fuck yeah! Dude slid on his KNEES to get a sword."

Paul snaps back, but his face glows. "Okay, that was pretty awesome, I'll admit."

And then Gretchen looks at me, "And, you? A pushover? Remember when you ran in after him?"

Ashley snorts. "Seriously. There was, like, no stopping you."

I sit up straighter. "Yeah. I guess I can be pretty hardcore." A smile that starts from the inside grows out. I can't stop it.

Dylan says, "Oh hells yeah!" And then does a flip in the middle of the café. Which is a super bad idea because he's bleeding from about a million different injuries. He misses the flip and splats on the ground. We rush to him like one flock of birds and lift him up. He groans but is laughing. And we're all laughing, too. But still, no one really looks at each other. We are shy toward each other, raw. Emotional sunburn not quite healed.

Paul leans into me a little and I lean in back. A tendril of hope has started in my chest, growing out. A tendril of something new. But then I'm aware of little arms wrapped around my leg and I almost kick back. I almost send the little wizard flying. He is hugging my knee.

He steps away and sniffs, wiping away a tear. "Wow, you guys. I didn't know it was so hard out there. That's some intense stuff." And then he pats the back of my knee.

DYLAN

Wizard dude is loooonneeely.

But then again, so is our sad little group. I remember our class on the outside and look out the window fast. But they've clearly rabbited now and it's just a view of a ramp and the gardens and the forest and shit. And the dark sky is back, twisting in on itself.

Demon dude must have given us just a glimpse of what we're missing.

What a dick.

"Hey," I say. "I wonder if we can break these windows?" Before anyone can answer, I throw a chair at the glass.

It bounces off and parts of it almost hit Violet, who—badass warrior-style—ducks. The chair breaks and wood splinters.

"Aw shit, sorry, yo," I say, cringing. Oops.

"I don't think the windows are breakable," says the wizard. Ashley looks at him with this look like, "Shut the fuck up," and the wizard sort of flinches. Girl can wither anybody.

"Well, I just don't think they are," he says under his breath, but loud enough for us to hear.

Violet, her hand butterflying around Paul's hand says, "I know we're not done here, but we should really think about going. Next are the doll carousels."

I let out a breath of air. More dolls.

Gretchen says, "We should grab weapons." We look around, and the chair I just broke has four great sticks to use.

"I've got my staff!" says the wizard, smiling at us all.

"Poor dude," I say. I pat the top of the wizard's pointy hat as I pass by to grab a stick. Something cold knocks against my leg in my pocket—the lighter. "Hey, we can make torches!" I realize I yell this and try to calm down. I know Gretch will try to rein me in in a mo. Or at least she would have before. I don't know anything anymore, truth be told.

Paul turns to me, his face lit up. "Is there anything in the kitchen? Like any beer or anything?" He looks to the wizard. "You were there. Anything in there?"

"Oh, I don't drink," says the wizard. He puts his hand up to his mouth like he's telling a secret, "Not a good idea to drink and wield a staff, if you know what I mean."

My lip twitches. There are too many good jokes. Just. Too many.

Violet answers him, "Yeah," like she really understands. But then says, "Did you see anything else, though? Like any type of alcohol—even rubbing alcohol?"

Because evidently Violet and Paul are of one brain now and seem to know what each other is talking about.

The wizard says, "Hmmm . . . No, I don't believe I saw anything like that in there. All I saw were high, shiny surfaces and a box with a red cross on it." He puts his hand on the side of his mouth again. "Must be a church, but not very welcoming, if you'd like my opinion. Dylan, did I hear you say something about a church?"

I mutter, "Too soon, dude."

At the same time Ashley yells, "First aid!" She hobbles into the kitchen and then comes out with a box and another towel. Real quick she wraps up her foot and Gretch eyes her the whole time. But not in a mad way. An appraising way. Like, almost the way she used to look at me. A sadness trickles through my veins, drippity drip. I shut off the sad faucet and swallow it down. Most important here? Gretch being happy. And, you know. Living through this House. Ashley opens up the box and sure enough, there is a bottle of rubbing alcohol.

"What are you thinking?" Gretch asks. Which is exactly what I'm thinking.

Paul says, "Something for bombs. Like putting alcohol and some rags in a jar. Molotov cocktails."

I look at him. "Dude. You know how to make a Molotov cocktail? Like from the mean streets of UC Berkeley?"

He laughs a big laugh and the rest of us snort. He says, "No. I just know alcohol burns. From all the damn bonfires the people in our high school throw."

Ashley raises her eyebrows. "So many. So pointless." They share a look.

Gretch, wasting no time, says, "Sweet. I'll find jars." She runs to the kitchen and finds baby food jars and towels. And three or four small knives.

She picks up a knife and punctures the top of a baby food jar, sticking part of the rag in the hole. Then she takes some alcohol and pours a little in each jar. The rest of us pick up knives and do the same thing. We're like some kind of commando force, starting a revolution. Actually, we *are* that. Exactly that.

When we're done, we have a bunch of potential bombs, some small knives, and chair sticks.

Violet attempts to adjust a towel around her head and ear. Paul reaches in to fix it, almost offhand. They smile at each other. There's light between them now. There's light in the air, light between all of us. It all feels so raw still, but . . . maybe . . .

Gretchen wraps the baby food jars in a towel and ties it to her belt. When she moves the jars tinkle-tinkle against each other—angels getting their wings. Except hopefully not the asstroll angels we've had to fight. She says, "I wish I had my monster bag still. But," she sticks her hip out and actually smiles, "I can make anything look good." Gretch is, like, joking. This is the freest I've ever seen her. And we're pretty much on our way to die.

Ashley looks her up and down. "Super true." She shrugs and gives me a little smile—I smile back. She's not wrong. And we have a major thing in common now.

She turns toward the door. "Let's go kick some ass."

ASHLEY

The fight with Gretchen sticks in my mouth like glue. There was so much I wanted to say. So much I fucked up. Now she'll never think of me the way I was hoping she would.

What am I thinking anyway? Girl is straight, girl is straight, girl is straight.

I wonder *how* straight she is . . . Is she bi-straight?

Violet leads the way out of the café and turns around to look at us. "Okay, we have to go through the cask room, again, but just one tiny part of it. And then I think it's the doll room." She brandishes her stick. "Weapons at the ready." When she gets to the doorway, she takes a deep breath and walks through, fast, onto the pathway through the cask room.

Right away, the voices start in, yelling things at us.

"They aren't very nice, are they?" I hear from behind me. It's the little wizard asshole, still following us.

Now, another day, I would have punted the fucker over a bridge. But I have decided to try something new. Being nice. Or empathetic or whatever. Paul's words, Gretchen's words, even Dylan's words. Violet. All of that is sitting with me funny, so that my world is just a little tilted. A little new. So I say, "Uh, yeah."

That's all I've got for now.

"Good luck, humans! See you in hell!" calls the ram from above the door, because rams are dicks.

Saints and statues all around fake-cry and point and laugh at us. "As if they'll win," a saint whispers to a taxidermied wolf.

The wolf laughs. "They always think they'll win. They always think they're different."

I try to ignore them, and finally we reach the door to the doll carousel room. I can see something turning in there, white lights bright next to red velvet.

We all look at each other and then take deep breaths. Then we step through.

Hundreds of dolls on towering carousels. Dolls with fancy dresses, old dresses, tattered dresses, new ones. They all ride small carousel animals, their faces fixed, frozen in smiles or just plain blank.

We start up the ramp.

No dolls move.

The wizard says, loud, "Was it this room you were afraid of?"

We all turn back to him and say as one, "SHHHHHH."

But then Paul whispers, "He's right. Nothing's happening in here. Why aren't the dolls moving?"

We hear scurrying overhead. As we turn the corner of the ramp, I catch a glimpse of another carousel. This one with other types of mannequins and figures. One is an outright devil, with horns and hooves and a tail. But nothing moves. We continue— into another hallway with a DOLLHOUSES sign above it.

I relax my shoulders. I didn't know I was tensing up.

"So we have to get through there at some point," I say loudly. My voice reverberates through the hall and I turn back around, half expecting the dolls to be right behind me. Nothing. Except the wizard. Who waves at me.

Violet stands up straight—we all seem to have assumed a Scooby Doo posture when we went up the ramp—and says, "Now it's dollhouses. And circus houses."

Gretchen says. "Just in glass cases?"

Violet nods.

Paul sighs and lowers the stick.

But Gretchen says, "Stay on guard. We have no idea what is in here ahead of us."

Violet leads us through the dollhouses. Lights flicker on and off. Dolls in the cases open their eyes.

Gretchen says to me, softly, "These must be like your house, Ash." But she's not being mean.

I laugh, even though I don't let anyone call me Ash. Gretch can call me Ash. "It's true." And it is. My house is freaking huge. Being the daughter of an asshole dad has its privileges. Lots and lots of them. Which could all go away if I tell him . . . As if reading my mind, Gretchen stays back until we're walking side by side and asks, without looking at me, "*Are* you ever going to tell your parents? What do you think they'd do?"

I sigh and jump a little when a doll smacks itself up against the glass.

"I don't know. Honestly. It's not just my parents I'm afraid of either. It's . . . everything. Losing everything. You know. This life I've built. Well, this lie I've built anyway." I look away, my gaze on the dolls in the houses trying to scare us, pretending they have a life, like anything they do is real.

Gretchen nods.

Then, because evidently hell has just frozen over, and pigs are flying, she puts her hand in mine. "If you want to, and need help, I'll be there."

My throat clogs with a lump. I don't know what this feeling is in my chest but it's hard and heavy and beautiful all at the same time. I swallow the lump down and stare at her, taking in her gorgeous eyes, the furrow between her brows. Her awesome hair. Her awesome awesomeness. I've lost words.

She smiles at me and winks. "I mean, if you want to add me to the mix. Like, 'Hey guys I'm gay, but worse, I'm friends with this girl. She's on food stamps.' I'll bring my monster bag. They'll love me." I laugh so loud I make everyone turn around. They give each other looks and then keep walking. Dylan gives us a sad smile but turns around and gives us space.

I hold her back a little and let everyone go on in front of us. I swallow and look her full on. "Friends?"

Gretchen lets go of my hand and looks down. She trains her beautiful eyes on me. They are soft. Vulnerable. My heart beats a little faster.

She says, "Honestly? I don't know. I'm . . . I mean, there's a lot to think about. And I'm with Dylan. Though . . ." She takes a deep, shaky breath. "I think we both know we're meant to be family, not together-together. But, mostly, I'm still getting used to not hating you right now. I have years of practice doing that, you know." She gives me a wry smile.

I nod, but I feel my stomach drop. That answers my next question then. Which was about being a little more than friends . . . But that was just a stupid thought anyway. A hopeless one. One I'm used to feeling since I knew I was gay when I was, like, a little girl: disappointment.

She takes my hand and squeezes it and then leans in and kisses my cheek, slow. Her lips are soft and I can smell her perfume. Something herbal and beautiful. She whispers, "But I'm not saying it's off the table."

Then she lets go of my hand and catches up with the others, falling in step next to Paul who points ahead of them. She nods at him, but then turns back to me and flashes a smile that makes my insides melt. What a tease. But for now? I'll take it.

I hear behind me, "You go, girl!" and look down at the wizard, who is holding up his hand for a high-five. I shrug, my smile so wide it hurts, and high-five him.

VIOLET

I'm walking next to Ashley and Gretchen with a satisfying repeating thought swirling around my head. *You suck, Mr. Rhinehart.*

If I get out of this House alive, I swear I'm going to . . . be mean to him, somehow. Oh, yes, I'll be mean.

Gretchen comes up to me as we walk past cases of tiny circus scenes that come to life when we pass—somehow we went from dollhouses to circus scenes—and asks like she was in my head, "Are you going to tell someone about Mr. Rhinehart?"

Ashley, who comes up on the other side of me, says, "If you don't want to tell anyone, you better do *something*." She nudges her elbow into me. "I'd be happy to help. I'm pretty good at making someone's life miserable."

I laugh and so does Gretchen. Hey. Gretchen laughed. Hey! They're smiling at each other.

But I snap back to the question, putting a finger up to my chin. "You know, I think I might just send a nice, anonymous note to the school. And to his wife. I don't want my parents to find out. They'd be heartbroken." The shame sword shoots through me again, feeling like it's ripping my insides out. I drop my finger.

"Hey," Ashley says, her voice soft. "They'd understand, you know."

I swallow down tears and nod. That's just something people say. They totally wouldn't. Gretchen says, "But I get it." Then she looks at me with her intense look, the one that scares the ever-living crap out of me. "You stop that man. He will do it again, you understand? He'll do it again. But more importantly, he hurt you. And he should pay. He's the one who should be ashamed, not you."

Ashley lets out a grunt of frustration. "I'm so fucking sick of being a girl sometimes, you know? Such skeezy guys out there, doing shady things, getting away with it." Anger boils up inside of me. Gretchen nods next to me. We are one line of angry girl. And we are terrifying.

Come at us, House. Come at us.

Dylan says, "Hey, chicas, slow down." And as one, we three turn around and glare at him. He steps back like he's been physically hit.

"Uh, sorry, yo. I mean, however fast you want to go is how fast we should go."

Paul's beautiful face is alarmed. He says, "You are all pretty."

Gretchen says, "Because that's how our worth is determined? By how we look?"

The anger spills out, even at Paul, so I say, "If we weren't pretty, would you stop listening to us?"

Paul says, "And smart?"

Dylan adds, "And, like, totally wicked strong."

Men. But Dylan and Paul are great people—I've seen it all through this House. And Paul is just dreamy. So I smile at them both and they smile back. We are looking at each other now, I notice. All of us. We're looking at each other. And I realize: I love these people. I didn't know them however many hours ago. And now I love them.

Maybe the House isn't so bad after all.

We reach a corner and turn in to a small anteroom.

And come face-to-face with one of the freakiest clowns I have ever seen in my life.

The thing is in a glass case, thank all that is holy, but has an oversized clown head and lifelike wrinkled hands. Its big red mouth curves into a smile. And then it starts laughing. The loudest, creepiest laugh that makes me pee my pants a little.

Bad House.

I jump back into Paul, who has jumped back and bumped into yet another glass case that lines the walls. The five of us are pressed against each other and the glass case behind us, staring at the clown.

Paul whispers, "Holy shit." And I just nod. He's right.

I say, "Perhaps we should go?" as the clown starts beating the glass case, laughing louder and sending chills down my spine.

"Yes," says Ashley. "Yes, let's do." And the five of us sidestep as one away from the clown and onto the ramp of the circus room.

Things are getting real again. Adrenaline spikes shoot up my spine.

The clown is so scary, I almost forget the larger room we are walking into. But then I hear the elephant's trumpet. And I scream and look up.

Towering above me, two elephants rise up on their hind legs, lifting the four or five women standing on them as well. One woman points to us and laughs. "Step on the little mice, Gunther," she says loudly, and I hear a loud crack as the elephant comes down and slams into the railing near us.

We don't wait around to see what happens next. We run up the ramp. Tusks skewer a wood wall to the left of us, right over our heads. Splinters and wood pieces rain down.

"Run faster!" Paul yells and we all dig in. Gretchen has Ashley by the hand, pulling her, as she runs on her bandaged feet, to go faster, and Paul pushes me from behind. I stumble a little and almost run over Dylan in front of me, and then we turn another corner of the ramp, moving fully into the room.

Music starts playing and I remember this room suddenly. I remember the nightmares I had after I saw it as a little kid.

The room holds what looks like a huge traveling caravan with ornately carved gold fixtures. A circus caravan. Inside are about 50 mannequins dressed in something like army uniforms with scary rubber masks of different faces on each one. They hold instruments like tubas and drums, trumpets and clarinets and cymbals. More circus women stand on the caravan, dressed in belly dancer outfits, just like the women on the elephants.

Worse, on the other side of the caravan, is another large band, this one seated like an orchestra. The men and women wear cheesy '80s evening clothes and hold flutes, violins, cellos, and French horns. Their masks range from presidents—Nixon, Bush, Clinton—to *Planet of the Apes* masks to normal mannequin faces.

When we run into the room, every single one of them turns their head and looks at us.

If my count is right, there are over 100 angry, restless people-shaped people who want to kill us.

Gretchen says, "Oh. My. God."

I'm not a believer, but right then, I pray to whatever might be listening, too.

Part V

THERE ARE SOME WHO VISIT Boulder House who understand. They walk through the House with eyes wide open, staring at its inhabitants, feeling the seething rage and despair boiling underneath and staring out of the eyes of the inanimate objects—the mannequins, the animals, the dolls. Some people refuse to even go in.

Over time, the legend turned to story and the story turned to whispers, but still the whispers survived, winding through the countryside, told late at night as a warning to scare children, as a ghost story around a fire.

The whispers said this: that the House comes alive when Maxwell Cartwright Jr. wants it to. They say that during certain times, when the dark magic is just right and the rage boils over and the stars cut the right angles through the sky, Maxwell Cartwright Jr. rises from the unknown. He rises in his true form, with a face made of nightmares, and looks around his creation, his curse. And, through the darkest of arts, he brings those souls he wants to him, to the House, to his game. Bending the very nature of the Universe to his will. To punish the world for its selfishness. Its abandonment.

They say Maxwell Cartwright Jr. never tires of playing.

Excerpt from pp. 206, *The Collections of Maxwell Cartwright Jr.*

GRETCHEN

There is a moment when nothing and nobody moves. The figures in the room stare at us. We stare back. Then, faintly, from far away, I hear that clown-of-my-nightmares laugh again. And then glass shattering.

And then all hell breaks loose.

An elephant bellows again and for whatever reason, the band with the cellos starts playing. They play a fast, circus-y song, tapping toes and moving heads. A guy at the piano says, "All right!" and goes to town on the keyboard.

A tusk breaks through the caravan from the other side, raining down more wood on us.

And we, like idiots, are just standing here. I grab whoever is next to me and pull and start running like my life depends on it. Since it does.

Out of the corner of my eye, I see a tiger jump at one of the marching band guys and start ripping him apart. Screams fill the air. Other band members get up and try to wrench the tiger off, but an elephant foot crashes down on the caravan and crushes half of it. Three women topple off, screaming, and I see masked band members wiggling like pin-stuck bugs underneath the crushed part.

The music starts to get more dissonant, notes thrown here and there. We are running straight to the part where the orchestra band is. The people—or whatever they are—begin throwing down their instruments and standing up, pointing at us.

The clown laugh sounds behind me and then an elephant back foot steps down in front of me, knocking Paul into the wall and sprawling Violet and Dylan farther up the ramp. I fall back on my butt and something grabs my hair and pulls me up, turning me around at the same time. My head screams in pain. The mini bombs I have smack me in the leg and clink together.

Right in front of my face is the clown's face. He laughs in front of my eyes and his teeth show, jagged and pointy, exactly like a shark's, like the demon's.

I scream.

He leans in to bite me. I squeeze my eyes closed because I have never been more terrified in my entire life.

With a half-laugh, half-squeal, the clown drops me. He backs up and feels his side where a bloodstain blossoms on his white jumpsuit, bleeding over to one of the pom-poms. Ashley stands next to me with a bloody sharp stick in one hand, her chest heaving. The clown looks up from his bleeding side and his eyes narrow, making the painted lines around them land over his eyebrows like devil horns.

"Fuuuuck," yells Ashley and grabs my hand and we turn around to run. The elephant's foot is gone now, but the ramp is splintered and one minute too late I realize we have to jump over the indentation. I try to stop myself in time, but I land in the indentation and feel my ankle twist. Ashley stops in time and waves her arms like a cartoon version of someone falling in, and behind her, I see the clown run at her, fast. Like supernaturally fast.

"Ashley, behind you!" I scream.

Ashley, in some sort of crazy martial arts move, bends down and turns around, putting her arms up so that she just catches the clown on his thighs and vaults him over her.

Right onto me.

I see white, red, and pom-pom coming toward me, but I am yanked up by my shoulders right before the clown hits. He smacks facedown on the splintered wood and torn carpet and doesn't move. Ashley jumps over him and the pile of wood in one fluid move.

Girl's got some moves. Even on her hurt feet.

Paul lets go of my shoulders and says, "Are you all right?" But we're interrupted by Violet's screams.

President George W. Bush has her by the hair with one hand and has another arm around her neck, squeezing hard. I see her face turn red.

I always knew he was an asshole.

Dylan fights with a *Planet of the Apes* guy farther up. More orchestra people are trying to climb up the pit at us. The elephant steps on another part of the ramp farther down and a split in the wood and carpet rips up to the very top of the room, right by the exit. The clown begins to move in the hole.

Paul is already rushing at the Bush mannequin. He reaches Violet and takes the stick he managed to hold onto and hits the guy squarely on the head. The guy releases Violet, who turns around and punches him in the stomach.

Ashley sprints toward Dylan and I limp forward. My ankle hurts like a sonuvabitch. But I look back at the clown, who is now getting up on his knees, and I swallow down all the pain because no way I'm getting caught by that nightmare again.

The piano guy jumps in front of me, and without thinking I rack him and he crumples to the ground. Dylan has stabbed the *Planet of the Apes* guy and we all reach him at the same time. He reaches in the towel still tied to my belt and grabs a mini bomb. With one hand, he grabs the lighter out of his pocket and lights the bomb fast. He throws it in the orchestra pit.

Nothing happens.

"Run!" He yells at us. The 60 millionth time one of us has yelled it at each other. And probably not the last.

We sprint up the ramp, Ashley pulling me along as I hobble, my ankle screaming in pain with every move, and we make it to the exit. I search the sides of the wall, my ankle throbbing. Panic bubbles up inside me. "There's no door," I say. "No door!"

More orchestra members are climbing out of the pit and now the clown is completely standing up, laughing and pointing at us. Band members are working themselves out of the caravan, too, mauled by tigers or not.

The clown climbs over the hole he was in and then starts running at us, faster than humanly possible.

I grab onto the person next to me—Ashley—and turn around to run.

And then the bomb goes off.

DYLAN

I have never run so fast in my ever-loving life. My lungs hurt. My arm hurts from the puncture wound from the whale room, which was, like, a century ago. My side hurts from where the *Planet of the Apes* dude punched me. My face hurts from whatever shit flew into it. I have blood streaming in my eyes from something. But that clown won't stay down forever and that clown ain't clowning—that's one scary motherfucker. And there's no door.

So, we, like, run. Again. Always. Gretchen hobbling next to me, her face pale, sweat running down it. Baby's in pain.

We run past cases of old guns that I look at longingly. But I know—just know—they would be too hard to get out and we don't have enough time. And there's no guarantee they'll work. So. We run.

Past more hallways, these with glass cases of ancient Mayan shit. Some more puppets that move and clack and chatter at us as we pass by, their faces grotesque masks made for scaring.

We run until we get to the knight room. The one I thought was so cool because it had these kickass knight scenes with knights doing knight-y stuff. Three glass-encased areas take up the room. One on each side and then a hallway that leads to the right. One of the scenes is just armor, but I see it start to move anyway.

The other two scenes are gonna blow. One has a knight and a scary-looking horse near a dragon that has been slain. Thank

God for small mercies—a slain dragon, yo. The other contains two knights having a duel. When we run into the room, they start at it like they had never stopped.

But the knight with the horse stares at us intently. He scowls, then puts his face armor on. And begins throwing himself against the glass.

Paul yells, "Run through, run through," because I am slowing down to watch this knight.

I speed up and we run past a case of jewels and replicas of the crowns of England. Ashley full-on stops at one of these and I almost run right into her. I stop just in time.

"Pretty," she says, and reaches her hand out.

"Cliché much?" says Gretchen, who grabs her arm to get going. Almost like old times. I hear a crash and then the clown laugh. This laugh makes me almost pee my pants. I run closer to Gretch and Ashley as they turn the corner.

Violet goes first, then Gretch and Ashley, then Paul, then me. Any minute, I expect that fucker of a clown to grab me. That's some Stephen King *It* shit. Not cool.

We run until we hit the next door. Then we all stop straight up. Through the door are the doll carousels. The other figurines. And the four horsemen.

Behind us are murderous band players and the creepiest soul-sucking clown you could ever imagine. And whatever else managed to follow us.

This, ladies and gentlemen, is being stuck between a rock and a hard place. We all sense what comes next.

I see Ashley look back and forth between what's behind us and what's in front of us. "Fuuuuck," she says.

Yep.

We look at each other.

Violet is crying, silent tears rolling down her face. Ashley's face is dead white, mascara and blood trailing down like sad rivers. Gretch's face is set and determined, but there is something else there, something sad-happy-calm all at the same time. Paul's eyebrows are furrowed and he looks back over his shoulder.

Ashley says, "I don't know why you're so freaked. This is so easy. We'll be back on the bus in just a minute, with some great stories." Then she laughs, but it turns into a hiccup-sob.

We all know that's not true.

We hear the clown laugh get closer. Hear a spiderwebbing crack of the knight cases.

A voice calls out, "Hey, there you guys are." Around the corner comes the wizard. That tiny fucking dude followed us the whole way. "I lost you all in that hubbub back there. Man, you guys are fast." He stands next to me and says, "Whew. What a scene, huh?"

Violet says, "I want you all to know . . ."

But then the clown comes around the corner, its laugh echoing through the corridor.

We run through the door.

PAUL

I am going to die without having kissed Violet. And this, more than anything, makes my blood boil.

The minute we run into the huge room, it's a mess of movement. Dolls start swinging from the carousels; there are swooping things, screams, neighs, yells . . . All the while, slow carousel music plays.

"Dylan!" I yell, "Bombs!"

He grabs a bomb from Gretchen's makeshift satchel, lights it, and flips around in midair to throw it at the clown. It hits the clown on the head and bounces off. The clown is knocked to the ground and the bomb lands by him. We run up the ramp of this room, right by the carousels, and the bomb goes off.

I feel something land on my head.

A doll.

I wrench it off, but just as fast, another one jumps on me, this one poking a finger in the gash on my forehead. I yell loud and yank that one off and throw it at a crowd of dolls gathering on the carousel. Just as I do that, another bomb goes off. The smell of burnt flesh and hair fills up the room. So does smoke.

I can't see anyone.

"Violet!" I yell. "Dylan, Ashley, Gretchen!"

I hear their screams from somewhere up ahead of me, but then something slashes my back. I feel air on my back and then the pain hits.

I turn around and a knight stands there with a sword, my

blood on the tip of it. He must have just scraped me. But that hurt enough. He swings sideways again and almost gets my stomach, but I jump back just in time.

I jump right on a doll and my legs get knocked out from underneath me. The knight looms over me and raises the sword straight up. I put my hand up to block it and feel someone pulling me from behind, just as something jumps into the knight, knocking him forward. The thing stands on top of the knight, its horn slightly chipped at the top and stained red with blood. A bent pole on either side of his back and belly. A bite mark on his neck.

"Sparkles!" I yell. He whinnies at me, and the person who grabbed me helps me up. Violet. She has blood dripping down her forehead, into her bangs, down her neck. Her face is painted with ash. She is a goddamn beautiful warrior goddess. I think I love her.

Captain Tidbittles canters up and stands next to Sparkles, putting a hand on him. Millie trots up next to him, carrying a doll arm that she uses like a baseball bat to smack another doll that jumps at her.

"Nice to see you, young sir. The battle goes on." The captain winks at me and points up. Angels sweep back and forth yelling banshee screams. I hear an elephant bellow somewhere and a tiger roar.

I feel a swoop of air and Violet yells, "Ow, you piece of . . ." but whatever she was going to say gets interrupted by Gretchen's scream up above us.

Violet's ear is now bleeding hard again, but she runs straight up the ramp and through the smoke, elbowing flying dolls as she goes.

A goddamn beautiful warrior goddess. Who is this girl?

I follow her, ducking dolls and angels. An angel manages to get my hair but I twist its arm away. A doll jumps on my back, right on the sword slash and I grunt in pain. Reaching back, I grab the doll's hair and fling that little shit far away from me.

I stop for a second. My back. The sword.

"Violet!" I yell, but it's no use. So I turn back around to the knight still on the ground. Captain Tidbittles and Sparkles aren't around and the knight is trying to get up. The sword lies by his hand. I am running so hard that when some doll lays down right in front of me, before I can stop, I go flying. I land right by the knight, the sword by my thighs.

A literal iron fist pummels into me, right into my kidney. The aching pain takes over everything and the sides of my vision start blacking out. I roll over just in time to avoid another hit. The knight can't seem to get up, but it can sure as hell still hurt. I get up on shaky legs and grab the sword.

"Fuck you," I say, and then add because I always wanted to say this out loud, "you cad!" and am about to plunge the sword into the knight's face when something smacks against my head. An angel.

I've had about enough of angels now.

When it swoops by again, I stick the sword up hard, right into the neck of the angel.

Angel this, you dirty dogs.

I'm thinking in Shakespeare and for one moment I feel the shame that shoots through me like it usually does, but then I realize that I actually don't care. It's what I want to think like. It's who I am.

I'm a badass knight for the good, motherfuckers. And yeah. I own a jerkin.

I spring up the ramp again, this time swinging the sword from side to side. I manage to get at least three dolls. The smoke is starting to clear and I get a better view of the top.

Gretchen is on a landing near a replica of a huge church, and she's fighting the clown, one half of his face blown-off and cavernous. Ashley is covered in dolls. I swing my sword around and cut dolls in half, left and right. Violet is almost to Gretchen, and I am almost to Violet—but before we can do anything, the clown plunges a stick in Gretchen's side. Blood spreads around the wound immediately. Her eyes go wide.

Both Violet and I yell, "NO!" at the same time.

I see Ashley's face, blood smeared everywhere, her hair hanging around the sides of her face with dolls hanging off of it. She screams a bloodcurdling scream.

Ashley grabs a doll on one side and flings it, then grabs the other one and flings that one. She shakes the dolls off of her feet and then takes a flying jump. She lands on the clown's back, then leans her head over and bites off his good ear.

Bites. Off. His. Ear.

This all happens in two seconds.

She yells, "GO TO HELL, CLOWN!" and the clown throws her off with both arms. She goes flying and lands on her butt. The clown stands there and laughs. But out of nowhere, Dylan jumps down and stabs the clown right in the neck with his stick. Its laugh cuts off and it croaks, "Uh-oh." And then falls sideways.

Everyone sprints to Gretchen. When we get there, she is lying down, her face white, eyes wide and scared. Violet grabs the towel around her head and ties it tight around Gretchen's torso. Dylan and Ashley fight off the never-ending doll onslaught. I stick my sword up and swipe at any angels.

Gretchen looks bad. And now I feel the fear in every part of my body. This is death. Hers. Ours. This is *our* death.

"Shit," says Gretchen, and laughs.

Violet says, "Shh. You need to get up. We have to get out."

I look down at Gretchen, who has tears streaking down her face. "Silly girl. I'm not getting out. You guys go. You guys go now."

Tears threaten my eyes. Not Gretchen. Not any of us. We're together now. All for one. Like Violet said. We're together now. An angel swoops down. I slash at it, and it flies away. I look up. The statues from the carousel above us have started moving. And these aren't dolls. These are human-like figures. Naked women with goat heads, horse's heads, Pan-like. There are at least two hoofed, devil figures. And they're climbing down. Toward us.

I hear horses whinny.

My stomach drops. Of course.

The four horsemen of the apocalypse sit on horses in front of the only exit. Guarding it. The band members and dolls are coming up the charred ruins of the ramp, the smoking doll carousel with more dolls climbing over it. I can feel the thumping steps of the elephants trying to make their way here. A tiger roars from somewhere. Angels fly overhead. The bombs we had lie in a ruin near Gretchen, glass broken everywhere.

Ashley says, "I don't think so," as she bodily lifts Gretchen up and drapes her arm over her shoulder. "I'm not done fighting with you yet."

ASHLEY

If there is an afterlife, I will not go to the light.

No, I will haunt the fuck out of dolls and clowns and angels and anything else that is pissing me off right now. Especially clowns. I almost can't wait.

Gretchen's sagging body makes me almost burst into tears. But then she kind of rallies and stands up, taking her arm off my shoulder, which feels cold after she does that. She looks ahead and behind and sees the situation we all see.

"Huh," is all she says, then sags again. Dylan catches her and she says, "Getting stabbed hurts like hell, I gotta tell you."

A doll hurtles toward me and I punch it in the head. It falls in a heap by my feet.

"Let's go," I say, setting my stare straight ahead. If an angel or a band member or an elephant grabs me, so be it. But we are heading straight toward those weird-ass naked goat-women and the devils.

I hear screaming and fighting behind me, though, and I can't help but turn around. We all do. Through the smoke, I can see them.

A voice rings through, "Go, young sir! We will keep them off!"

Paul yells back, voice choking, "Thank you for everything, Captain Tidbittles. Sparkles." Then he turns back around and swallows. He holds the sword with both hands. He says to us, "We go down fighting. We go down together."

Violet, looking fierce, nods next to him. "Fighting and together," she says.

I say, "Duh." And for one second, everyone laughs. I give myself one small smile.

"You got Gretchen?" I say to Dylan. He nods. I take a deep breath. "Well then, let's kick some ass."

We walk toward the chaos ahead. Angels swoop at us, but Paul manages to swipe almost all of them.

The freaks come fast. A woman with a goat's head comes charging at me.

I will say, here and now, that a woman with a goat's head is terrifying.

The head chomps at me and I grab her by the arms, but still she manages to chomp a clump of my hair and rip it out.

I punch her in the boob, and I hear a goat bleat. While she's distracted, I see a panpipe on the ground and I pick it up and smack her in the head. She falls backward, back into the carousel.

I look over at Gretchen, who is leaning against the wall but still slashing at things with a knife. She stabs a doll and shakes it off her knife, then sags a little. She holds her side and doesn't notice that one of the hoofed devils is stomping toward her.

"Gretchen!" I yell, but there's a black and orange blur as a saber-toothed tiger jumps at the devil and grabs him by the neck. A strangled, wet noise follows and I see the tiger tear out the devil's throat. The tiger looks up and around, right at me, then turns its gaze to a woman with a horse head. The tiger jumps at her and slashes her dead in half a minute.

I officially love tigers.

More figures are climbing down off the carousel and I run over to Gretchen, who is just below the exit door. And I see them for the first time—the four horsemen. They stand there, terrifying, wind moving their cloaks, horses pawing the ground.

Dylan, Violet, and Paul run over, too. Hundreds of figures now, climbing down from the carousel. Mermaids, demon horses, more small devils . . .

I sigh. This is it. There are too many to fight off now, not enough to help. I sag against the wall near Gretchen. Paul puts up his sword and Dylan his stick. Violet growls—the girl growls!—and faces the figures coming toward us. But I can barely breathe. I just hope it doesn't hurt.

And then I see the pointy top of a hat come through the fog ahead of the figures.

"Goodness," says a cheery voice. "Well, this won't do. Not if you want to get out of here."

It's the wizard. We all stare at him dumbly.

He rolls up his sleeves. "Allow me. This may help." He raises up his staff and blasts a white light right into the gang of assholes coming at us. Everything blows up, shooting devils and demons and dolls all over the place, knocking us back hard against the wall. I'm inhaling smoke and coughing like crazy, my eyes streaming tears. But as the smoke clears, I can see that he laid waste to pretty much all of them. There are bodies and twitching limbs and groans, but they are all down.

I will always, always, always high-five tiny wizards when I see them. Always.

Paul, looking as happy as I feel, says, "'The fire-eyed maid of smoky war/All hot and bleeding will we offer them.'" He shakes his head and says to the wizard. "You awesome bastard, you."

The wizard beams. "Well, thank you! You all remind me of past days, you see. You seem so close and I used to have a tribe like you, but I lost them. And I have been just a tad lonely—" Before he can continue, an angel swoops down and picks him up and drops him in the cavernous pit where the carousel used to be.

I am suddenly filled with rage. That asshole hurt our wizard. No one hurts our wizard!

The angel swoops back around and I get ready to pounce. When she gets close enough so that we can see her stupid face, Paul raises his sword and Dylan his stick. I crouch down—

But then she drops from the sky with a knife in her heart. She lands at my feet.

We all turn. Gretchen smiles at us and says, "Suh-weet. I didn't think that would work . . ." Then she holds her side and groans. The red on her shirt is spreading.

I say, "Nice shot." She winks at me and my heart explodes. I hold onto the moment as long as I can.

It's so quiet now, it's almost peaceful. But we all know what's next. Like we choreographed it, we turn around to the door.

The Horsemen stand there, huge and gray.

Violet takes a deep breath. She looks at us all and says, "Well. Should we face the apocalypse now?"

Part VI

ONE LEGEND SAYS THAT MAXWELL Cartwright Jr. lost once.

A few years after the House was finished, a world-renowned poker player came to town, arrogant and sure, hearing of this terrible House and the man who never lost. When he arrived with his entourage of bodyguards, admirers, and hangers-on, he appraised the House and all that was in it. And he wanted it.

He challenged Maxwell to a game. Winner take all.

If the poker player won, the House and all its treasures would be his. If Maxwell Cartwright Jr. won, the poker player would be in his debt forever.

They say the game lasted seven days and seven nights. That the two stared at each other, daring the other to call his bluff, neither giving an inch.

But in the end, when the poker player laid down his cards, a malevolent glint in his eye, Maxwell Cartwright Jr. saw . . . the House had lost.

They say the Earth shook with his rage.

Excerpt from p. 236, *The Collections of Maxwell Cartwright Jr.*

DYLAN

Gretch is hanging on me and I feel her body shaking. That douchetroll clown. I hate that motherfucking clown.

But no time for thoughts of vengeance because we're not done. We are walking right up to the apocalypse mofos. Gretch makes little whimpering noises. My heart whimpers with her.

I look back in case anything is coming after us—we're the caboose after all, Violet and Paul ahead, us three behind—but the room has disappeared.

Like, gone. Nothing.

Just gray empty space.

The four horsemen of the apocalypse are ginormo in front of us. I can't see any of their faces. Their cloaks move though, like there's a breeze or something, somehow.

Fuck-a-doodle-doo.

Gretch lets go of me and Ashley. She wobbles for minute, Ashley and me holding our hands out in case she falls, but she gives us a smile and stands on her own. The whole right side of her from stomach on down is a horror movie. I turn to the horsemen so she can't see the tears.

I don't know if Gretch is going to make it. And a world without her . . .

White hot anger shoots through me. "Get it over with!" I yell at the horsemen.

Violet reaches back and finds my hand and squeezes it.

My voice echoes—off what, I don't know. One of the horses

paws at the ground, but it's silent after I yell. Then, the rider on the end horse steps down, leaving the cloak in the shape of a human. One long, spidery-ass leg slips down and then the other. Red eyes. Top hat. Cane. The cloak on the horse falls.

Demon dude.

Paul stands up straighter and says, "So you're one of the riders of the Apocalypse?"

The demon laughs and it echoes all over the place, bouncing off of itself. "Oh, these guys? Props. They mean nothing." He waves his hand and the horses and the dudes disappear, like dirt blowing off cement. Their gray colors streak, and then there's nothing. Now it's just us and this demon. He looks at me. "Sorry to disappoint, John."

I can't help it; I flinch. Four years hiding that name in front of Gretch and it's just out there now. It feels weird. And wrong.

Ashley sighs and gives a grunt. "Yeah, yeah. Whatever. Can we do our, like, showdown or whatever? I mean, whatever it is you have planned for us? You know, clowns or dolls or gigantic whales . . . Whatever your serial killer wet dream is, you pathetic loser." She's got tears on her face and she glances at Gretch. She's thinking the same thing I am.

But still: don't taunt the demon, yo. Still I gotta admit the girl's got balls. Or ova, as Gretch would say.

Demon dude looks at her, eyes swirling. "Whatever, indeed." He takes his cane and twirls it around, yet again walking around us. His smile stretches across his pale, nightmare face.

Violet says, "We made it through. We made it through together." She shifts on her feet and then says really small, "So we beat you?"

Demon guy streaks to her side, so fast it makes MY eyes twirl.

"Not quite, V-i-o-lated." The thing smiles again, but I see something in there. I see something behind his weird-ass twirly eyes. I see fear. And rage. Paul moves closer to Violet—almost on top of her.

But seeing that demon's fear has made me strong. I stand up straighter. "Yo, we beat you. Give it up. Let us out."

"Let us out" repeats in my head over and over and over, like the words are running around us, chasing themselves, until the phrase is just a hiss.

When the last hiss finishes, demon dude stops looking all casual and then stares at me, this time his eyes cavern-black and his mouth curled up to show his teeth. I step back a little. Okay, motherfucker is still scary. I move closer to Gretch who leans into me a little.

He stands up straight and then leans on his cane, a nonchalant look pasted on. "I'll admit—I'm big enough to admit, you see—you have come further than I thought possible." He looks around at the nothingness. "Further than any I've . . . played against." He taps his long fingernails against the top of the cane. "But you have one more test, my dears. One more test. And then we'll see how much you 'stick together.'"

I groan and it echoes through all of us. I'm so tired I can barely stand up. And Gretch . . .

Paul says, "After this test, we're done, right? We win or lose, nothing else."

The demon bows. "You have my word." And then he laughs again and claps his hands together like a little kid. "Oh, but this is a fun ending. I'll be so happy to put you in my collection after such a hard-won fight. This makes you so much more valuable to me. Your fall so much more delicious, much more than I anticipated."

His laugh is still ping-ponging in my ears when he gets dead serious again. "You see, where you are going now is so much worse than here, you'll be happy to get back to the House."

Gretch and I look at each other, eyes wide. Ashley grabs Gretch's hand. Paul and Violet step back into us so we're like a standing doggy pile of scared.

The demon cocks his head at us. "But I'm afraid I must wipe the slate clean, so to speak. So that you know exactly who you are in the end. You will see, my dears, you will see. You are the same people as you were when you walked in."

He stands tall in front of us and then? The motherfucker grows. We all tilt our heads back and watch. Paul throws his arms out like we're in a car and he's the seatbelt. As if that could remotely stop this dude.

"Behold," he says as he looks down. "The last test." He claps his hands and the white light erases everything.

GRETCHEN

It's like I fell asleep. In the middle of the hallway. I blink and look around.

Well, I'm still here. In the nightmare.

High school.

Students are milling all around and the slam of lockers is so loud it makes me cringe. I shake my head to try to clear it. I feel fuzzy and strange. Maybe I'm getting a migraine. Where the hell is Dylan?

Ashley Garrett walks by me and stares. Something in me pulls. My side hurts and I have no idea why—I feel so weird I look away from Ashley without even insulting her.

Weirder—she didn't insult me.

Trent walks by with his basketball, twirling twirling twirling it. His eyes look funny, but maybe it's just my weird vision right now. I get a quick flash of a crow for some ungodly reason and then it's gone. Trent's walking with that Paul kid everybody loves. Paul looks at me and I feel another tug. His eyebrows furrow.

Where is Dylan?

The bell is about to ring and I try to remember what period it is. I look to the person next to me, whoever it is. "What's the next period?"

The girl next to me stares and I look her in the eyes. She seems familiar but I can't remember her name. She's rubbing her ear. "I don't know," she says. Making this weird-ass day even weirder. Maybe she's on drugs. Maybe I am. Jesus.

I slam my locker and look around. No time for this, whatever's happening. I have to go home after school and check on my mom.

Finally, I spot Dylan's backpack bouncing through the hall and I run after him, knocking people out of my way. My fur boots are somehow wet and I forgot my monster bag, but I need something—someone—familiar. Someone I know inside and out to make this strange feeling go away. I catch up to him and grab his arm.

"Dylan! Where have you been?"

He turns around and his eyes are scared. I instinctively put my arm around him and feel my eyebrows furrow. "What's wrong, babe?"

He just shakes his head. "I don't . . . Something is just off, yo." He mumbles it into my neck like a secret and I take my arm off. I feel it, too, but I'm not complaining about it. We just need to forget it. Survive. Pretend everything is okay.

Trent walks by again with the basketball. He's gotten so good at carrying that thing around that he only uses one finger to keep it twirling. In fact, he's not even using his other hand to move it. His eyes flash at me and I do a double take—why does my mind keep flashing to a crow? Something runs down my spine and for whatever reason my side aches again. But right then, someone yells, "John Luke!"

Dylan's eyes go wide; he's terrified. I look around to see if something is coming—he looks that scared—but all I see is some girl walking toward us. I try to look him in the eye, but he's looking around the hallway, like for an exit. "What?" I say. "Do you know this chick?"

She comes up to us and I check out her outfit. It's like *Little House on the Prairie* only way more conservative.

Dylan backs away from me and the girl. "Dylan!" I call.

At the same time the girl says, "John Luke! Are you coming to church tonight?"

It seems like the whole hallway stops. I look at Dylan and he's shaking.

"Babe. What the fuck?" I say. Because now this scared thing is contagious. And who is this chick? And what is going on? I shake my head to try to clear it. The edges of the hallway are blurring out, like an old-timey photograph.

Dylan tries to get through the crowd, but Trent stands there with the basketball, still spinning it. Paul right by his side with a confused look on his face. That same pull happens. I get a picture of a sword in my head and then it disappears. The girl tugging her ear is beside him and now a flower flashes in my head and I'm not sure why. Purple.

"Dylan?" Now my body is shaking. The hallway is quiet. Dylan and I are somehow now in the middle of a circle of students and it feels like everyone is staring.

The *Little House* chick walks up closer to us and says, "Hey, John Luke? Are you embarrassed of God?" A wicked grin crosses her face. "You'll burn in hell you know. For lying."

I back up a bit. "Dylan. What the fuck is going on?" I stare into his cloudy stormy eyes.

"Babe," he whispers.

ASHLEY

Kaleigh whispers in my ear, "Oh my god. The freaks are fighting."

Then she and Madison laugh into each other's shoulders.

Something doesn't feel right. For some reason, I don't want to stand here and stare at Gretchen and her boyfriend like the rest of these dumbasses. Seems pointless. And . . . something else. And also I can't remember how I got here. Fugue state much, Ashley?

"Let's just go," I say and turn around. Right into Jane. She stands there and smiles at me. Like a fucking wolf about to eat a rabbit. This isn't right. This isn't how it goes. I'M the wolf.

"What." I say, hard. "Get out of my way."

To the right of me, in my peripheral vision, I can see the ball on Trent's finger spinning and spinning and spinning.

Jane says, "Where are you going, Ashley? Off to meet someone?"

Her smile grows wider. And then my panic sets in. It's like she knows something. And NO ONE knows anything. She couldn't know anything, right?

I swing my hair back. "Per usual, *Jane*, I have no clue what you're talking about. I just don't think these people are worth my time." Something is wrong with me. I can't seem to make fun of Gretchen and Dylan. This sort of situation used to be my dream, but I can't think straight. I muster it up and say low and hard, "Get out of my way, loser. Or you will be sorry. If I wanted to see freaks, I'd go to a carnival." The words taste like acid in my throat. I roll my shoulders to get the ick feeling out.

But Jane doesn't budge. She leans in closer to me and tickles my ear with her breath. "Do you think I'm pretty, Ashley?"

I yank my head away and step back, right into Paul. We look at each other for a second and I see a flicker in his eye. I feel it, too. We both squint at each other, like we're trying to figure each other out.

Because we are.

What is it we know?

"Hey, Ashley, do you think *Gretchen* is pretty?" Jane asks. Her smile travels up her face, like too far up her face? It reminds me of something. Something fucking awful. I shiver and sweat starts down my back.

Now Kaleigh and Madison are looking at me. In fact, it feels like the whole circle is looking at me. Jane walks forward and I walk backward. She walks me backward until I'm standing by Gretchen and Dylan, who have stopped fighting and are looking at me. I can feel my fists clenching and unclenching, but it's like I'm not in control. It's wrong. All wrong.

"Well, do you? I mean. It's pretty obvious you're in love with her."

The sweat trickles down my back and I swallow. I swivel my head, left and right, the hallway blurring. Everyone is looking at me.

Trent's ball is still spinning.

Jane goes on, "Well go ahead, tell her you love her. It'll be a big romantic gesture, right?" She starts laughing.

And then Kaleigh says, "Holy shit, you're gay? Ewww."

Madison steps back from me. "Oh my god, how many times did you perv on me in gym class?"

The whole crowd starts laughing, except Paul who looks confused. And the other girl right by him, rubbing her ear and looking confused, too. Whatever her name is.

Violet.

Her name is suddenly there. I'm sure of it. It's Violet. And I know her.

But Jane is still coming at me. I have to do what I do best. That's it. Deny, deny, deny. Survive. Because everyone would believe me. I still rule this school.

I. Still. Rule. This. School.

Jane looks at me. "Well? Come clean. Are you a lesbo or not? Come on. Go ahead and give me a kiss."

I open my mouth to speak.

DYLAN

I do not know what's happening. Somehow the chirpiest girl in the world is backing down Ashley Garrett, the bitchiest bitch in the world. Except it doesn't feel right to call her a bitch. I don't know. Things are fuck-a-doodle-doo-doo right now. Something is wrong, yo.

Ashley's in the middle of the circle with us now. And the fuck? What's this about her being gay and in love with my Gretch?

Before I can noodle any of this—that repressed chick, Rachel, outing me; Ashley going girl-love and digging on Gretch—Rhinefart pushes his way through the crowd around us, standing by Violet. Something creeps down my spine. Something about Violet. Like, first of all, how do I know her name? And something else, too. I want to hug her and I don't know why.

Rhinefart's smile is super extra creepwad. He says, "What's going on here?"

Jane steps up by Trent, his douchetroll ball spinning spinning spinning. She says, "Oh, quick recap, Mr. Rhinehart: John Luke here was telling his trailer trash girlfriend, Gretchen, that he's been lying to her about his name and other things. And then Ashley was just about to come out to Trailer Trash with a profession of love." She laughs. "It's a pretty good day, if you ask me."

Gretch next to me, speaks up. "Trailer trash? Really. Like you fucking know me." But the dig is weak. My Gretch can normally kick back hard. I can't think of anything to say. I got nothing. Just this stupid feeling that something is off. Just this helpless feeling. I'm forgetting something. Something important. Something that'll help here. I put my hands on either side of my head and smack smack smack. I need to remember.

Someone in the crowd yells, "Freak," again and I know it's for me. I feel itchy all over.

Rhinefart laughs. "Well, don't let me stop it." He cocks his head and looks at Gretchen. "Didn't I see you at Walmart using EBT?" He looks over at Jane. "I am so sick of subsidizing moochers. Good God. Do what you want with them."

I stare at him. Even Rhinefart isn't THIS bad of a teacher, right? Gretch shakes next to me and holds her side. She bends over. The crowd has started talking now, a million voices buzzing around. It gets louder and louder and louder and I put my hands over my ears. Gretch does, too, and Ashley looks around like, WTF, yo?

But then someone clears his throat and the buzzing stops. Paul steps forward.

He'll make things better. I don't know why I think that, but I do. I just know it. Know he's a good guy.

But all he says is, "Uh, I need to go to class," pulling his backpack closer to him. But he doesn't move.

"John Luke! Are you going to answer me?" That girl again. What is she doing?

Gretchen looks at me, "Why the fuck is she calling you John Luke, Dylan? How do you know this girl?"

"I . . ." I look around and swallow. The whole crowd seems to be leaning in. Gretch's eyes are hard. Ashley Garrett looks at me, waiting to see what I'm going to say. Paul clears his throat again and that Violet girl looks like she's going to say something. I stare at them all, looking back and forth. I'm alone in this, turns out. It ain't getting any better.

And I have to survive, yo.

"I have no idea, babe. Girl's messed up."

And the hall goes crazy.

PAUL

I don't know why, but I can't seem to leave. I can't stop looking at Gretchen and Dylan and Ashley in front of me. And I can't stop my skin from crawling every time I look at Trent's spinning fucking ball. I feel warmth beside me and know it's Violet. But on the other side of her is Mr. Rhinehart, the worst teacher in the world who super creeps me out. He's like Angelo from *Measure to Measure*—someone sleazy and awful. And he's not doing anything. He's supposed to be the adult. And he's not just standing there. He's egging them on, even.

When Dylan speaks, the whole crowd goes nuts. I have no idea what he's said because I'm thinking about the book in my backpack and how I need to get out of there and to my locker before anyone sees me. In the corner of my eye, I swear I see a flash of red as Trent's ball spins. How is he keeping that spinning? I look at him and he smiles, his smile traveling across his face for a second in a way that makes me step back.

Right into Tracey. And somehow my backpack falls and my books scatter, the Shakespeare sonnets sliding into the middle of the circle, right by Ashley's feet.

The crowd goes quiet again. And someone shoves me hard. I trip into the circle with Ashley, Dylan, and Gretchen. I reach for the book, sweat dripping down my temple, but Ashley picks it up. She looks me in the eye.

Then Tracey, who was bending down by my backpack, stands up, holding my Medieval tights.

How did they get in there?

Oh, god. Oh, god, no.

She holds out the tights pinched between her thumb and forefinger. She stands on the other side of Rhinehart. Who for some reason is standing really, really close to Violet. Like, crazy close. Violet looks like she's trying to shrink into herself.

Tracey says, "What. Are. These. Oh my god!" Then she starts laughing and pointing at me. Everyone else starts laughing and pointing at me, too. Except for Violet, who is trapped in the crowd and is now under Mr. Rhinehart's arm.

What?

But I don't have time to think about that. Ashley Garrett has picked up the sonnet book. Somehow, the laughing dies down and again it feels like people are leaning in. Ashley clears her throat and looks around. She hands the book to me and looks me in the eyes.

My face is wet—I realize I'm crying. Super brave man, Paul. Well done. Your dad would be proud.

I take the book and she stares for a second and the pull I feel is huge. But it's hard to think about that when I just want to run away, get the attention off of me. And in that split second, I can see in Ashley's eyes the same thing. My heart sinks.

She laughs loud. "I always knew you were a dork," she says at me. And the crowd starts laughing again. Then she turns to Jane, "And like I'd ever like *Gretchen*, Jane. She's on food stamps. If I were a lesbo, I'd have way better taste. Poverty pie really isn't my thing."

Gretchen's head snaps back like she's been slapped.

I clutch the book to my chest and try to grab the tights from Tracey, but she starts throwing them through the crowd and they bounce from person to person, each one saying "ew," and "gross," and "loser." The tears are back on my face.

Gretchen turns to Ashley, "Like I'd ever like *you*, you whore." Then her eyes flash at Dylan. "And who the fuck are you, Dylan? Who's this girl?"

The girl in the long skirt smiles a super creepy smile. "John Luke here goes to my church. His parents and my parents are best friends—both our families live in the Meadowlands community, far away from your *hovel*. We live in God's shining light, Gretchen. John Luke and I are going to get married after high school." She puts her arm through Dylan's, but he backs away from her and she steps back into the crowd.

Gretchen's eyes flash. "Is this true, *John Luke?*"

But Dylan swallows and then points. I follow his finger. He is pointing to Violet, now in front of Mr. Rhinehart. Who has his arms wrapped around her. He whispers in her ear and she looks at me with her eyebrows furrowed.

Dylan says, "Look at that. I think Violet is doing it with Rhinefart."

VIOLET

This is all wrong. Everything is wrong. I know these people. These people in the middle of the circle. I'm forgetting something. What am I forgetting? I look at Trent and the basketball spinning and spinning. I feel Mr. Rhinehart's breath in my ear and listen to his words, "You are nothing without me. No one else can love you. You are lucky I even noticed you. I'll be tired of you soon, though. It won't take long. You don't matter. No one will believe you, no one will listen to you." His words stab my ear with every syllable, to the point where my ear actually hurts. He says the same things over and over and over, like he's not a real man, but mechanical or something.

Well, he's definitely not a real man.

When Dylan points and the whole crowd turns their attention to me, Mr. Rhinehart's arms tighten around me.

"Ew, gross. What a slut!" I look to my left and it's Stacey and Laurie. They start laughing and backing away from me. "Don't get your slut on me!" Stacey starts laughing so hard she looks like a donkey.

Laurie says, "Seriously disgusting. He's, like, a hundred years old. But, really, you guys are a perfect match." She leans into Stacey and they snort-laugh.

I stare at them, barely registering their words. What am I forgetting? The ball flashes in my peripheral vision. I'm forgetting something important. I need to remember.

Ashley and Dylan and Paul and Gretchen look at me, then look anywhere else, their faces pale and stricken.

They are scared. They don't catch each other's eyes. Dylan won't even look my way. I don't know if they even know my name. But everything in me says I know them. I know them. How do I know them? What am I forgetting?

The whole school is laughing at me.

But so much weirder: I don't care.

Because of the thing I'm forgetting. It's there, whatever it is. It protects me. It means that none of this matters.

Remember, Violet. Remember.

I feel my spine get straighter. Remember.

I feel power build up inside me, I feel it push goosebumps out.

The power grows, bigger and bigger, until I can barely swallow. I take Rhinehart's hands and pull them down and off of my body. And then I step forward.

The crowd is still laughing, but the laughter sounds weirder. Forced.

I am calm.

I look at Rhinehart and say, "No."

The voices around me get louder, but I say again. "No."

I stare him down. I stare everyone down. I look them in the eye and I burn it into them. "No," I say.

The voices taper off and suddenly it is dead silent. Then I hear it: click, snap, whir from somewhere. The sound echoes off the lockers.

Click.

Snap.

Whir.

I've heard that sound before. Somewhere, a million years ago. It stirs something in me. It mingles all around this new power I have, this new me.

I say it again, this time louder. "NO." This echoes off the lockers and down the hallway. A million Violets saying a million nos.

Rhinehart steps back and snarls. "No one will ever love you. Who do you think you are?" His words multiply and ricochet all around me.

Who do I think I am?

Click.

Snap.

Whir.

Who *do* I think I am?

Remember.

I am a fucking ninja-goddess-warrior.

And I am waking up.

An image flashes through my mind, a man in a bed, sleeping, a demon flying out of a clock, a skeleton in a closet. Trent's ball spins spins spins in front of me.

A laugh starts in me. I step forward into the group. They are all looking at me.

"I know who I am." And now the laugh grows bigger. A warm feeling spreads through me. I know these people. And they know me. We are not alone.

"Who do I think I am? I am Violet," I say to the group in front of me. A flash of something—a cane, a top hat, the man in the bed sitting up.

Click.

Snap.

Whir.

The voices around us start up, buzzing softly but then building louder. I squeeze my eyes shut then open them. Remember. Remember, Violet. More flashes: dolls, a whale, running running running, Dylan doing a flip. The man in the bed sitting up.

Remember. Remember, Violet. Wake up. WAKE UP, VIOLET.

And there it is.

I open my eyes and look at my people in front of me. "Wake up," I say.

Click.

Snap.

Whir.

Ashley stares at me and swallows. She's almost there. I say softer, "Ashley. Wake up."

Something shifts in her eyes. She stands up straighter, no longer looking like a hunted animal. The voices around us get louder. She shakes her head, as if to clear it. Then she turns to Gretchen, "I am Ashley fucking Garrett," she says, like she's just realizing it. Then she turns to the crowd. "And I *am* gay." Then she smiles big. "And I do like you, Gretchen. Fuck it!"

The voices get louder, sounding angry now. Then she adds, her smile growing bigger, "So suck on that, bigots!" Kaleigh and Madison and Jane hunch together. Flashes of crows on a branch pop in my mind. But then: Ashley throwing her shoe, flipping over a railing, catching Dylan, her feet mangled. Tears have started in my eyes.

Click.

Snap.

Whir.

Wake up.

Gretchen stares at Ashley. Then looks at me. Her eyes are clear and determined, the Gretchen I know. She grins and slaps her knee. "Oh hells yeah! I am Gretchen, you assholes." She turns to Dylan and chokes up a little. "I don't care what anyone says. I know who you are. Who gives a shit about these people?"

I am almost doubling over now, laugh-crying. These people. These beautiful people. And I remember Gretchen fixing Ashley's feet, throwing her knife at an angel, fighting the clown. Tears pour down my face.

Dylan stands up straighter too and then lets out a whoop. He hugs Gretchen who starts laughing, too. "I am motherfucking Dylan in the motherfucking house, motherfuckers!" He spins Gretchen around and Ashley laughs and I laugh. He turns to the crowd and says, "I remember. I remember, you douchetrolls!" He grabs Ashley's hand and Gretchen's hand. I remember, too.

Dylan beating away dolls, throwing the bombs at the circus people, wrapping his shirt around my ear.

I turn to Paul, swallowing, hoping hoping hoping.

Wake up, Paul. Wake up.

Click.

Snap.

Whir.

He puts his hands on my cheeks and leans in, a huge smile on his face. I stare into his gorgeous brown eyes and I know. I know he knows. My face hurts, I smile so hard. He says, "I am Paul. And I remember. I remember, Violet." I hiccup-sob and a snot bubble comes out of my nose.

But I don't care. Because we're awake.

We woke up.

We smash into each other, hugging in one big mess of a group and Gretchen and Ashley and Dylan all saying sorry sorry sorry and laughing and crying and the voices around us are getting deafening now. I can even hear the spinning of the basketball whirring around us.

I remember. Our test. Our last test. High school. Life.

I break away from the group and say, "Wait. One more thing." I walk to the crowd of people, Rhinehart and Trent in front of me.

I square my shoulders and say, "We're awake, motherfuckers. Fuck all y'all." And then I punch Rhinehart in the face.

VIOLET . . . (REDUX)

A person could get really used to swearing.

But before I can decide on that for a lifestyle, the moment I punch Rhinehart, the high school walls disappear and we're in the House again. Only, it's started twirling like a carousel. The whole thing, with us in it. I see a hole open up in the floor and things start to slide into it, like we're in a giant toilet bowl and things are getting sucked down.

The demon stands by the hole, his clothes moving in the wind that is picking up. His face is furious and his eyes twirl like crazy. He is terrifying. The spinning picks up and I can feel my feet slide on the floor.

Paul grabs onto a shelf that is bolted to the wall and I grab on to him. I feel arms around my waist that I'm sure are Dylan's. The room is spinning faster now and the wind is whipping my face. My feet are barely on the ground. I can just barely look up and when I do, I see something that makes my heart stop.

The door. The door to the outside. And it's open. I can see the gardens of the House and the sun shining down. I even get a glimpse of some students from the high school milling around. Something flies past my head barely missing me. I duck down but can't stop myself from smiling. Now my legs are totally off the ground and I'm holding on to Paul's belt for dear life.

The outside is right there.

We're about 20 feet away from it if we crawl along the wall

holding on to the shelves. Five staggered shelves to the door. I yell to Paul, "Outside door!"

He yells, "What?"

I gather up my loudest voice, my "NO" voice and yell again, "Outside door! Ahead." I see him look up and nod. Then he starts pulling himself and all of us along the first shelf. I keep my eyes on the outside door. Paul makes it to the second shelf, his arms shaking. I wonder how he can do this at all with his arm bitten by a tiger. My love for him grows times a million.

There's nothing I can do to help. Paul has all of our lives in his hands. I squeeze my eyes tight and whisper to myself, "Come on, Paul, come on, Paul." I think all the hero thoughts I can at him. Brave, beautiful Paul. Strong Paul.

I hear Ashley yell from behind me, "Hey, Asshole Demon Thing, we won! This isn't fair!"

A voice booms all around us and rings in my head. I almost let go of Paul to cover my ears but stop myself just in time. The voice says, "The House. Always. Wins."

So. He's a bit of a sore loser.

Paul has reached a third shelf, but I feel Dylan's arms slip down my waist. "NO!" I yell, but hands grab my feet and I know he's caught onto me. My arms are burning and I don't know how long I can hold on to Paul. I wonder how Gretchen is hanging on. Nothing feels lighter so I think we're all still here.

Paul's grunts reach me through the whirlwind. He inches up the third shelf and reaches for the fourth. I close my eyes.

For a minute, we're airborne, but then there's a tug on my already burning arms, and I look up and we've reached the fourth shelf.

Hang on, hang on, hang on. I'm shaking all over, trying with all my might to not. Let. Go.

The fifth shelf is a shadowbox type thing that is even with the one we're holding on to. A tiny marionette holds onto the edge of it, but when Paul reaches it, the marionette gets swept away, its tiny growl just barely audible.

We have just the door to get to now. Paul crawls along the shadowbox and reaches his hand out to the doorframe.

But before he reaches it, I feel a release from my feet.

Dylan isn't hanging on anymore.

PAUL

The release is so sudden, I almost let go of the doorframe, but I hang on and pull, my muscles screaming at me. Without the weight, I pull so hard, Violet and I tumble to the ground right by the outside door.

We're standing in front of the door, the whirlwind in front of us but totally not touching us. Behind us, there's a shimmer across the exit like the one we saw at the entrance. We're in some weird bubble. Not outside but not in the whirlwind either.

Dear Paul of however many hours ago: why the fuck did you go through the shimmer? But actually, I don't feel that bad about it. Not now. If we can all make it out, that is. No way am I leaving these people.

My heart is hammering and not just because of the pulling. I squint into the whirlwind, but I can't see anything but colors twirling.

Violet looks at me, panicked.

I know, Violet. I know.

But then, I see a hand grab onto the doorframe. A hand with black fingernail polish. And then the matching hand. Two hands on the doorframe and then just a giant whirlwind. Both Violet and I don't hesitate—we grab onto those hands and pull.

We pull Dylan out of the mess, and attached to him is Gretchen. We all fall down into a big pile. Dylan stands up, but Gretchen is on the ground, holding on to her side.

Dylan grabs my shoulders. "Ashley."

Violet stares wide-eyed. "What happened?"

Gretchen cries on the ground, her voice weak. "She let go of my legs. When we hit the doorframe. I don't know what happened."

Dylan and I say at the same time, "I'll go get her."

Violet smacks both of us. "No! I'm going!"

Gretchen looks up and says, "I'll go."

She struggles to get up.

And all three of us snort at her. Just as I'm about to throw Violet back, so she can't go and get hurt, and plunge into the whirlwind myself, I see a beautifully manicured hand covered in blood grab the doorframe.

ASHLEY

That cheating asshole.

The thought keeps going around and around my head. And it is this thought and the idea of ripping that demon thing's head off that makes me strong enough to grab the shelf once I let go of Gretchen's legs. It is this thought that pulls me over shelf after shelf until I get to the doorframe and grab onto it, my arms shaking, my breath coming fast.

That cheating asshole douchebag.

When my hand hits the doorframe, I get pulled hard and I land in a heap on top of Dylan, who is on top of Paul, who is on top of Violet's legs, who is next to a laughing Gretchen, still holding her side.

I get up and pull Dylan up, then Paul, then Violet, then Gretchen.

I look at the shimmery exit in front of me. Then look at the rest of my people.

The outside. This is the outside.

I squeeze my eyes shut and then open them again. It's still there.

THE OUTSIDE.

Without speaking, all of us grin at each other. We grab hands like the freaks we are.

Violet is in the front and says, "Let's get out of this fucking House."

Love me a girl that swears.

We step through the shimmer.

VIOLET

I hear birds chirping and a breeze tickles my cheek. Paul's hand is strong in mine. The sun is shining.

We're out.

Ms. Harper is about 15 feet away from us, texting on her phone. She looks up briefly and says, "We're just waiting on a couple others. You guys can go to the bus," but then she goes back to her phone.

We look at each other.

There's nothing on us. I feel my ear and it is whole. No blood, no nothing. Gretchen's outfit is nonbloody and everything is dry. We don't have scratches or anything.

All five of us let out a huge whoop and hug each other in a tight huddle.

Dylan lets go of us and does another flip, this time landing it perfectly. He yells at the House, "Take that you douchetroll House!"

Ms. Harper looks up. "Dylan! Language."

But we are all laughing so hard we ignore her. Paul stops laughing suddenly and says to Ms. Harper, "Uh, have you seen Trent around? And a spinning basketball or anything?"

She furrows her brows and looks at him like he's crazy. "Paul, Trent isn't even on this trip. Why? Did he sneak in or something?" She looks around like he could pop out from anywhere.

Paul shakes his head. "No, never mind."

I can feel in my gut, though, that we are out. Truly out.

We won.

We woke up and we won.

Paul comes over to me and shrugs. "I had to check." He grins and his awesome brown eyes sparkle.

I say, "Hey, I don't know about you, but I want to get out of here, like right now." I motion toward the exit door. "Just in case."

Ashley says, "Amen."

At the same time Dylan says, "Hallelujah." I grin at them and they grin back. I notice all three of them holding hands and wonder how this whole thing is going to work out.

And just for a second, I pause. "Things are going to be different now, aren't they?" We all look at each other. I see the students by the bus, can hear a girl scream laughing and can see a guy chasing her. Most of them are on their phones. I can almost hear the dramas playing out with all of them. I can almost hear all of them afraid.

They look so . . . small.

We've been taken apart by the House, put back together in different formation. A part of each other now. Together.

Ashley breaks the silence and snorts. Then she takes off her shoes. "Uh, yeah. Thank fucking god."

I laugh and so does everyone else. But it's a deeper laugh. Because things *are* different now. New. I don't know how this shakes out from now on. None of us do.

However it does, though, I know we'll be okay. We woke up. We won. We're here. Together. It's going to be okay.

I smile bigger.

And with that calming, awesome, amazing thought drifting in my head, I take Paul's face in my hands and I bring him down to my lips. And I kiss the hell out of this beautiful boy.

I know who I am. I am Violet.

I am a badass warrior.

I am a righteous ninja.

I am a hero of a revolution.

I am a beautiful warrior goddess.

And I am not alone.

THREE WEEKS LATER, THE POKER player disappeared. No one knew where he went or why. A search for him lasted for months until finally it was called off.

One year later, the man's suit, covered in blood, was found in the woods around Whispering Bluffs, Wisconsin. A note was pinned to it, written in rust red, tracing out a symbol and four words. A crow's feather sat just to the side of it.

The note, the legend says, read only:

The House always wins.

Excerpt from p. 314, *The Collections of Maxwell Cartwright Jr.*

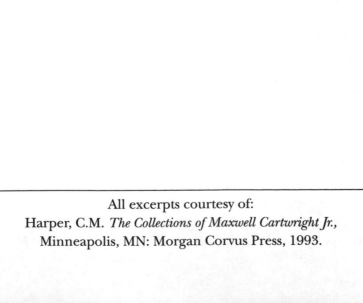

ACKNOWLEDGMENTS

This book was a labor of love and there are SO MANY people to thank. Like, so many.

First, my agent Ammi-Joan Paquette, who took a chance on me and signed me as a client. You guys, AMMI-JOAN PAQUETTE! Can you believe it? I still can't. Joan championed me through several drafts, the brutal submissions process, and the mountains of neurosis that come with this territory. Joan, THANK YOU.

And of course, my editor, Dan Ehrenhaft, also took a chance on this weird little novel—y'all he's so good. Dan is the best. Believe me, I know how lucky I am. I'm so grateful for all your work, Dan! And for your answering, with patience and aplomb, every single email I sent you. Always. Guess what—YOU'RE the talent. And can we extend this thanks to Soho Teen and Soho Press? I can't recommend them enough (I'm looking at you Rachel, especially, and Meredith, Paul, and Abby, too). Such a brilliant, savvy, kind, welcoming group of people.

A huge thank you to my beta reader, T.J., for doing a phenomenal job and for letting me know what's what. T.J., you are a superstar and a brilliant reader and I think you should read everybody's stuff. You're fantastic—thank you!!

My writing group, Molly Beth Griffin and Katie Behrens read countless drafts of this manuscript. They helped me polish and polish and polish this baby and never complained ONCE. They probably know these characters as well as I do. Also, they are phenomenal writers. PHENOMENAL. I adore you, kittens. Thank you.

Alicia and Jeremy Jepsen were kind enough to house me while I did research and Alicia even, super sweetly, hung out with me. Thank you, thank you!

Patrick Blomquist also had a hand in helping this book come to be. His sister, Cathy, and her family also very kindly let me use their cabin for an uninterrupted week of writing madness. So awesome. Thank you to all of you and the whole family.

Laura Ruby, you read this book when I was in a panic and gave me the best effing advice. On top of it, I adore you, did you know that? You are brilliant and amazing. The same words describe you, Christine Heppermann. I will forever and always be grateful you both are in my life. I hope you're reading this while sitting in my apartment and drinking wine with me. If not—come over, both of you. I'm totally not busy. Bring Anne. More on her later.

Speaking of amazing friends . . . Dear reader, while I was working on this book, I had the worst year of my life. The worst of it was when my mom passed away. It is not hyperbole to say that I could have easily drowned. But the beauty, support, and kindness of the people around me kept me from getting pulled under. These people held me together while my world came apart. Anne Ursu, Megan Vossler, Natalie Harter, and Jenny Halstead became my life support, along with Brett Kallusky, Patrick Jones, Jordan Brown, and Pete Webster. You darlings, you amazing people, do you know how you saved me? Do you know how precious you are to me? I hope so. You are in my heart, always and forever. I love you all. Not even a move across the country is going to change that.

Add to that amazing group Sharon Kahnke, Shaun Murphy, and Sarah Tiller-Holman—we became friends more than 20 years ago and you are still my family. I love you so much. This path wouldn't have been possible without you. You are a part of me. Sorry, if you ever hoped to get rid of me. It just won't ever happen. Every step of the way you have been there and every step forward we'll walk together too. You're beautiful souls and I'm so grateful for you.

Which brings me to Anne Ursu. You all. Did you know an angel walks among us? I know one: her name is Anne Ursu. Besides being a BRILLIANT writer and teacher, she is one of those people who just brings good into the world. She IS goodness. I've watched her quietly and consistently work behind the scenes to bring opportunities and success to people and to entire movements. I've watched her move in this world and make it constantly better. (Not to mention, she has basically worked as my career manager because she's so smart and kind, and because I lean on her for everything.) She makes the world a better place every single day. I love you, Anne. Thank you for being my friend and for being who you are. The world and the children's lit community are better because of you.

And finally, speaking of family, I need to talk about mine. As I said, I lost my mom, which still breaks my heart every day. She was an English teacher for 35 years—a thankless, hard, and never-ending job. And she LOVED it. She gave me a love for words and she believed in me. She never once doubted that all my winding roads would lead to the right path. She never doubted I could become an author. I wish she could see all her hard work pay off. Mom, I hope you're proud of me. I'm always and forever proud you were my mom. I love you and I miss you.

I have often wished my dad could be everybody's dad, because everyone deserves the love and support he brings. He is the kindest soul I've ever met and I aspire to his level of good everyday. Dad—I love you. Thank you thank you thank you for being my dad and for always making sure I have a net of support.

My brother, Scott, and my sister-in-law, Marlie, have been founts of support, too. Not to mention my awesome and brilliant nieces, Brianna and Colette. I love you all so very much!

And! I'm almost done, promise. A few others to name: Beth Brezenoff, for reading this and making me feel good about it; Rachel Adams for sticking with me through everything; Mary Rockcastle and the MFAC program at Hamline—Reader, if you want to write? GO THERE! The MN kidlit community for being an AMAZING and one-of-a-kind support system for the fantastic breadth of talent in the state. You are all the best.

And to you, dear Reader: thank you. You're the reason this book exists.

It's embarrassing to have this many amazing people in my life. One person shouldn't get all these riches. But I'll take them. Also, if you've read this far and you're not someone who knows me personally, you deserve something, amirite? Write to mcatwoodauthor@gmail.com with the subject line "FINISHED" and if I can, I'll send you a haiku about a unicorn. You've totally earned it.